In loving memory of Mel Reisner and Sherry Martin

Dedication

This book is dedicated to:

My wonderful husband who has supported my dreams for years.

My four children, Brenna, Kylee, Taryn and Jack who have been my biggest cheerleaders.

~Chapter 1~

The September sun beat down hot and hard as I trudged
slowly across the back edge of the football field, far from the school
but close to the practicing players. I looked up into the blistering
blue sky and wondered if the Arizona sun would ever cool down or
if this would finally be the year of 100 degrees every day. It was
foolish, I knew; Phoenix never cools down much until late fall, or
whatever passed for fall in this sun-blistered state, but after a
summer of record-breaking heat, I was at the end of my rope. I had
stayed past the last bus for French Club, but I wasn't sure if getting
the participation points in French class was worth the effort of
walking home after. Actually, I was sure it wasn't. And if I hadn't
had an ulterior motive, I might have dropped the club entirely. This
train of thought was derailed by the sounds of physical exertion that
roiled wildly in the molten air.

Mammoth Stadium was at the northern edge of the school. I
hated the name and our school mascot in general. No matter how
many times I saw it, the sight of the furred face with comically long
tusks next to the name Phoenix High never got less ridiculous. On
my first day, the far too enthusiastic student guide explained that the
first student body had voted for the wooly mammoth mascot because
they figured that only a genuinely studly mammoth would be able to
make it in Phoenix. Great logic, ancient and dumb scholars; I don't
think anything with "wooly" in its name could survive in this hellish
heat. Heck, I'm barely making it in a t-shirt and shorts. Adding to the
idiocy of it all, no one knew what a mammoth sounded like, and
there's certainly not a sensible school fight song for an extinct Arctic
animal fighting in Sonoran heat. But here we are, and here I was,
passing under the enormous, insane entrance sign.

The stadium itself was far removed from the aging cream-
stucco school building. Its only connection to the actual edifice was
the concession stands and ticket office, which nestled next to the
building, huddled in the glorious shadow it cast. The bleachers
followed, cement on the home side and metal on the away side, both

of which retained enough heat to burn unsuspecting spectators at the start of games. A black asphalt track ringed the field just in front of the fenced stands, shimmering lazily in the full sun of late afternoon. Behind the field where I was walking was a slatted chain link fence to keep anyone from watching the all-important high school games for free and, beyond that, a large area of empty grass.

Further along, so far away that the iridescent screen of a heat mirage warped its planes and edges, lay the main road leading to my apartment complex. It seemed miles away; I knew it would have been much more pleasant to walk across the easement between the tall brick school building and the towering cement bleachers, but it would have put me uncomfortably close to my actual goal. My eyes weren't fixed on the road to which I was, in theory, headed, but instead on the part of the football field closer to the concessions; there I saw the oval strip of black asphalt, which, for the moment, was home to a dozen girls in shorts and tank tops and the grassy green field in the middle, where dozens of boys practiced football in the searing heat.

Although it was definitely the green field that held my reason for this walk, I was still drawn to search for the homogenous group of girls, all blonde hair and blue eyes and California dreams, for the one that ruined my dreams. But in a sea of ubiquitous perfection, Tessa Austin stood out. Her perfect olive skin shimmered in the heat, a mirage unto itself, so smooth and brilliant I was sure she'd never seen a pimple in her life, at least not on *her* face. Dark chestnut waves spilled from a perfectly perky ponytail in cascades, not a single hair out of place, not even in this godforsaken heat. But it was her eyes that irritated me the most and drew the most attention; instead of the dark brown that would have normally completed her look, Tessa had the same bright green as my own. But where mine seemed to highlight the lack of color in my face, Tessa's glowed the dazzling green of an emerald caught in a field of tawny silk. Seriously, how the Gods of physical beauty doled out their wares was a little unfair, or a lot unfair, depending on the day.

Then, of course, there was the gaggle of girls surrounding her. I knew that they couldn't all be best friends, but it sure seemed like it. I watched as Brenna Tyson wrapped an arm around Tessa. Brenna was a tall blonde with deep chocolate eyes, and although she didn't catch the eye as easily as Tessa, she did manage to stand out in that crowd. They bent heads together over Tessa's phone and laughed easily. Another blonde, Charlotte Casing, peeked between their cheeks slyly, and all three giggled together. It was a scene out of a teen movie that wouldn't even have a side character like me, and it seemed just as surreal to me. I turned my attention to the other group on the field and the other end of the spectrum of humanity: the football team.

I watched closely as the football players ran through their drills, hitting each other, running plays, and then finally, at the coach's long-awaited whistle, collapsing onto the metal benches on the sidelines, tossing their helmets on the ground and guzzling water like they had been crossing the Sahara for the last week. This time was the part of their practice for which I waited and slowed my already tortoise-like pace. I searched close-cropped heads for the strawberry blond hair I knew so well, even as I kept a surreptitious eye on the cheerleaders practicing on the track. Tessa Austin must never know how I felt about Sean. I had never had a run-in with the chestnut-haired cheerleader, and I didn't want to start now.

I caught sight of Sean's head as he threw it back to chug something from a plastic bottle. He was so effortlessly handsome that it seemed unfair to every other guy in the school. Of course, that was only my opinion, mine and Tessa's, anyway. I tore my gaze from Sean and found Tessa at the top of the pyramid, arms pumped in the air and face filled with so much excitement it was as if they were cheering for an actual game. Yeah, that fits. The cheerleader, the football player, and the geek watching from the sidelines. Strains of Taylor Swift's "You Belong with Me" played in my ears; I shook my head to clear the earworm. We could be our own after-school special; of course, one of us would have to have an inaccurate eating disorder or an errant alcohol problem.

I stood and watched a little longer. The idea of getting caught watching felt less pressing than drinking in the sight of Sean. He was just under six feet tall, with blue eyes and a head of dusty hair that almost matched the landscape. Not many guys could pull off a head full of reddish-tinted hair without bringing coke-bottle glasses, overalls, and a goofy cowlick to the party, but Sean did and did it well. He was everything I had ever looked for in a guy, except for the annoying addition of his perfect girlfriend. Two peas in their mirror-opposite pod, Tessa Austin as perfect in her alluring looks as

Sean was in his All-American. I actually hate the phrase "all-American," but when you look like a walking Ken doll, I suppose you have to live with the comparison. I studied him a little bit longer and then decided that with the reddish tint darkening his hair, he was more of an Alan. I chuckled to myself. Dang, I was funny sometimes. I watched Sean until he put his helmet back on, then I decided I'd wasted enough time and should head home.

Since my mom had started working, part of my new daily routine was taking care of my younger brother after school. Although not riding the bus home afforded me the opportunity to ogle Sean, it also shortened the amount of time I had before Mike got home. And I was supposed to greet him at the door with a smile and a plate of cookies, or at least a grimace and granola bar.

I exited the stadium through the gap in the chain link fence at the north end of the field, grateful that the maintenance crew wasn't as concerned about people sneaking in as the booster club. We lived two miles from the school, far enough to be bussed but close enough that my mom had told me if I wanted to join a club, I was going to have to hoof it home afterward. She was a real estate agent, and times were tough. There was no coming home early to pick up her kid from school. She stayed late and went in early and fought for every client who walked through the door, just like the rest of the agents. She tried to be understanding of my interest in learning a new language, but she told me she couldn't lose her job just because I thought I might leave the country one day for a place more exotic than Rocky Point. So I had to make sure I was home in a reasonable time to watch Mike. My mom was a generally nice person, but between the recent divorce, the new apartment, and the new job, she had become a little less indulgent to her demanding teenage daughter.

As I walked, sweat gathered on my forehead and back and ran down my legs in small rivulets. "It's nature's air conditioning at work," my mother would say whenever I complained about the heat and what it did to me. The trouble was that I felt no cooler. I was glad that Sean couldn't see me, as I'm sure I didn't present the sparkling picture I saw in the mirror on a good day. Rather than the sleek curls of a magazine model, my red hair had gone limp and frizzy, a combination that didn't even look as good as it sounded. My pale skin was probably beet red and blotchy, the closest thing my Irish skin did to tanning. I didn't need a mirror to know that it was unlikely this look was going to steal him from the cool, tan, unflappable Tessa. I don't usually mind my Gaelic heritage, but the scorching, melting days of Phoenix did everything but highlight my best side.

I glanced up at the sky again, praying for a cloud to block the sun, at least during part of my walk home, but I didn't see any of the fluffy sun covers. I was just about to scream curses at the furnace gods when something caught my eye. I stopped walking and stared in disbelief at the vibrant blue expanse. What I saw didn't make any earthly sense. It was a rainbow of such brilliance that I could see the entire spectrum from red to violet in High-definition color. It seemed so solid that I felt for a moment that if I could just climb on top, I'd slide to the pot of gold at the end.

I looked around to see if anyone else had noticed the multi-hued arc in the sky and was startled to realize how far I had come. I was standing nearly in the middle of the grassy expanse that spanned the distance between the stadium and the road. I was not startled, however, at finding myself alone. It was too hot for casual walking, and no one besides another student would be walking here anyways. Assured that no one else could confirm my sighting, I turned back to the sky. As strange and wonderful as the rainbow was, I found myself wondering if it could be seen from everywhere on the ground or just where I was standing. I'd never seen anything like it before, and maybe that was because it was a sight specific to this spot, not visible from any other angle, or maybe it was just the beginning of sunstroke. It held me transfixed, and I was afraid that if I moved, it would disappear.

I stayed still as long as I could, but the sun was relentless. I started walking again, and the rainbow did not disappear. As I walked, I found my gaze returning again and again to the brilliant arc in the sky. Then something even stranger started to happen. The arc seemed to be truly bending toward the earth as I walked; not just the illusion, but it was actually growing bigger as I neared the curvature. For the first time since I was five, I thought about trying to find the end of the rainbow. I knew it was a fruitless task, that the mirage of an end was always just beyond the next house, but this time, I could have sworn the rainbow's arc was getting closer to the ground. The bright colors seemed nearer and just as solid and tangible as they had in the sky.

I didn't even stop to consider the wisdom of my actions. My life in the past few months had been a series of disappointments and despair. My father, apparently divorcing my brother and I at the same time as my mom, had left Arizona for a job back East. I know the reality was that the job was good, and with his company downsizing here, it had been a smart move. My head knew all of this, but my teen heart longed for my dad to talk to me, take me places, and tell me I was pretty, even if Sean Flannery never noticed. But he had gone, taking his new and pregnant 23-year-old girlfriend with him. My mother's work meant that she was never there either, and of course, there was the Sean thing going on, or not going on, as it were. That was on top of all the usual sixteen-year-old crap that everyone has to put up with. I wanted, no, I *needed*, the end of the rainbow.

I followed it for ages; I knew it was farther than two miles because I passed my apartment complex about a half hour before the arc seemed to take a nose dive straight for terra firma. I stopped in the weed and cactus-choked empty lot behind the neighborhood grocery store. I thought it was extremely possible that I had sunstroke or heat stroke or had been stung by a scorpion somewhere along the way. The rainbow came to an end in the far corner of the field, tucking itself neatly in the corner of a rotting, bleached wooden fence and flaking stucco wall. It was quite a sight, the almost solid, sparkling, brilliant colors coming to rest among plastic bottles, beer cans, cigarette butts and other assorted trash.

"Mary-Claire, you really are going nuts," I said aloud, and my voice sounded strange and hollow in the heat-soaked air.

I had found the proverbial end of the rainbow, but it wasn't a proverb, and I was standing within yards of every child's dream. I started toward the corner slowly, my feet firmly crunching the assorted refuse on the ground; the sound of it juxtaposed with this otherworldly vision and possibly the only thing that kept me connected to the real world. With every step I took, I expected the multicolored sight to dissipate before my eyes and leave me looking insane, idiotic, and disappointed once again. As I neared the end, I put my hand out to touch the rainbow, and, to my surprise, it felt…sparkly. Kind of like a pleasant electrical jolt; I withdrew my hand, and the sensation stayed for a second or two longer. If I was nuts, my hallucination had taken on a multi-sensory aspect, and for a second, I wondered if I might not truly need to see a psychiatrist. And then I was sure.

Sitting at the end of the rainbow, where it had no earthly business being, was a largish black pot shining in the desert heat and brimming with gold coins. I had officially lost it. I wondered idly if my mother would feel the least bit responsible when they found my overheated body in the field, as clearly my mind had taken a holiday and left something weird in its place.

I reached for a piece of gold, wondering if it would feel cold, hot, or...sparkly. I was so wholly absorbed with this latest happening that I didn't notice anything else in the lot.

"Hey there, skitter, no one said you get to keep me gold!"

~Chapter 2~

I jumped about four feet up and back simultaneously. And even as my heart beat fast enough to bruise my ribs, my brain found time to wonder what a "skitter" was. I knew I had gone insane. I knew it like I knew that there's no actual end of the rainbow, like pots of gold don't exist at the end, and like I was going to be so painfully sunburned from a long hike in the Phoenix sun. And yet, as I looked toward the impossibly black pot which seemed to hold sparkling gold, only one of those knowns in my life actually seemed certain.

"Well, I'm not going to bite ya. I just was telling you that you don't get me gold," the lilting voice said, sounding amused at my confusion. Why was my hallucination sarcastic?

I looked around wildly, my eyes darting from one dust-choked cactus to the next, but they found nothing to latch on to, no person who would be talking to me in an Irish brogue, as though a random stranger talking to me about how I didn't get their gold would make sense. When I finally focused on the seeming source of the voice, I wondered why I decided to fixate on a hallucination. There was a man standing next to the pot, leaning casually against it. He was no taller than six inches and dressed from head to toe in green. Green leather-looking boots with a bright gold buckle front and center on each one, dark green/light green striped tights that led up to green knickerbockers, and a green vest barely able to stay buttoned over a protruding belly. A green shirt buttoned with tiny gold buttons, a green bow tie, and a green top hat with a black rim and large gold buckle completed the look. The only thing not green on him was his ruddy face and fiery whiskers and hair. It was the Lucky Charms character come to life. And he was sweating, which, for a vision, seemed an odd detail.

"Why don't I get the gold?" I asked and found the question to be absurd, although given the current circumstances, absurd seemed like the way to go. Also, it was the only one I could think of. Well, I could think of about fifty more, but they all fell under the headings of "Really?", "*Really?*" and "Are you real?"

The little man threw back his head and laughed louder than I thought someone his size could. "My goodness. In all me years, and there have been quite a few, never has anyone opened with that question. I believe they all wondered it, but no one has ever asked it, at least not first."

I stared at him, unsure of what to say next. He stared at me as though willing me to ask something else. As I looked into his green beetle eyes, I found myself thinking my original question had been reasonable. I had discovered the end of the rainbow, so I was pretty sure the gold was supposed to be mine *if* I knew my superstitions, which, I confess, it was possible I didn't. I must have won the standoff because, after a minute, he cleared his throat and smiled at me again.

"Well, since that be your first question, lassie, I'll answer it first. This," he said, gesturing grandly to the pot, "is *my* gold. I've earned it and the right to keep it. I'll not be sharing with you."

"What do I get then?" I felt somewhat rude with my questions, but I'll admit the whole situation had shocked the polite right out of me. My brain was functioning on the most rudimentary level. Breathe, pump blood, and say whatever pops up first; no societal filters on. And I wanted to know what I got for fulfilling every child's dream. Certainly, there had to be something more than a conversation with the world's smallest man.

He eyed me carefully, and I noticed his eyes were the color of emeralds and just as brilliant. They sparkled, but I did not see any joy or sense of humor there. As we stared each other down, his gaze softened, and the hardness slipped away; now, his eyes reflected warmth. I was more confused than ever, and the heat was relentless. I wiped the sweat away and kept looking at him. I still had nothing running through my brain but my original query.

"Ah, that'd be the second question then, eh? No thought to asking me name? Or sharing yours?" he said, his lilt tempering the sharp reproach in his voice.

I blushed then, finally coming to my senses enough to realize that this unearthly creature had better manners than I did. It's a bit disconcerting to realize that a manic vision was more courteous than oneself. And I wondered why in the world I felt my mirage was so out of my control.

"Hello, I'm Mary-Claire McColl. And you are?" For good measure, I smiled at him.

He smiled back at me, and I didn't detect the coldness in his eyes this time, but I wondered if it was still lurking underneath, like a crocodile in a mud hole.

"Ah, a proper Irish name to be sure. Me name is Larry. And *you* have found the end of me rainbow." He followed this last proclamation with an expansive motion of his arms, taking in the rainbow, the gold, and the dry, dusty, dirty scene in which it was all placed. He seemed absurdly proud of this fact, or excited, or something.

I nodded as though all he said made perfect sense. It didn't. I wondered if I should ask my second question again, or if I should think of another, or if I should just stay silent and see what Larry came up with; I chose the latter. Larry and I started our staring stand-off again.

He eyed me for several seconds, then a smile crinkled his eyes and puffed his cheeks. "You're not the most talkative of your kind, are ya? Well, I guess you'll be wanting the answer to the second question then. And I'll be answering. You get me."

Suddenly I couldn't think of anything to say. I felt the heat of the sun burning the skin on my arms and the back of my neck. I smelled the unpleasant odor of rotting food, superheated dirt, and a little bit of my own body odor. Rivers of sweat ran down my neck and back, and even worse, into my eyes; I could feel an uncomfortable and disgusting paste beginning to form on my feet where perspiration was meeting dust. I was tired, hot, and slightly dehydrated, and I was no longer amused by this little scene. I looked at him to see if he was joking, but only serious green eyes looked back at me.

"You?" I wasn't sure what that meant, and I wasn't sure if I wanted the grand prize from this little adventure. Maybe, if I were in first grade, it would make a terrific show and tell, but I was pretty sure the novelty would wear off pretty quickly, and then what? In first grade, indulgent smiles from my teachers and the uncomprehending adoration of other 7-year-olds, but in high school?

A one-way ticket to a padded cell and psychotropic drugs for life. Yipee....

"Oh Mary-Claire, it's not what ye be thinking. You don't get the fortune of me forever, just until you've wished three true wishes."

I blinked slowly, turned, and took in the empty lot, the sound of the grocery store's air conditioning unit humming somewhere not too far off and the sunlight catching the shards of broken glass scattered around. I looked up into the sky and was nearly blinded by the white sun. I heard the scrabble of something on the hard, hot ground. I moved my foot slightly and felt the prickle of a cactus spine. Then, since I could still see the magical objects, I deliberately pushed my ankle into the cactus spine. It hurt...a lot...so I assumed it would have the same effect as a pinch and wake me up. I tore my gaze from the desert scene around me and returned it back to the rainbow, the pot and little mannikin standing next to it. So the "pinch" did not work.

I felt like I had stepped into an alternate reality without leaving my normal one. I kept trying to decide which reality was the one I should focus on, but they were so intermingled that I wasn't able to pick one. With my brain heat-strangled and my energy sapped, I decided to accept this was all real for now, so I looked around expecting to see something else incredible, like a blue genie popping out of the pot and singing my three wish rules.

"Three wishes? Anything I want?" I asked. If this was going to be my new life, I decided not only to accept it, I was going to jump right in. Now, with the teen angst jumble that was my life, what to wish for first... I opened my mouth to speak my first wishing opus when Larry grabbed my hand and made sure I was paying attention.

"Yes, but three true wishes—there is a difference, and I'll be knowing it," he said, keeping his gaze on me.

"What do you mean by true?" I asked. He had repeated this phrase twice now, and I felt that it carried some import with it.

I was surprised when he only smiled and shook his head. "I could try explaining it to ya, but I don't think you'll understand. Just know, you can wish for whatever ya want, and I'll know when the wish is true."

"Ah, so I'm back to anything I want," I said, deciding to ignore the whole "true" thing. If he wasn't going to explain any better than that, then I didn't need to bother trying to figure it out.

"Well, o'course there are rules, but I'll be telling you about them as you wish."

I started for a moment. "Wouldn't it be easier if you just told me what they are now?"

His smile grew bigger and somehow more sinister, though it changed in character not at all. "Easier, to be sure. But I've been granting wishes for a long time," he said, pausing to look at the black pot and the gold coins spilling out. "And easier is not always the most fun."

I shook my head slightly, wondering if I wanted this and if anyone had ever refused. I doubted it, though. Even without the singing genie, I still wanted my three wishes, three *true* wishes. During the whole conversation, my brain had quietly been knocking with its own question, but my mouth was too busy saying anything it wanted. Now that it had calmed down, the question first in my brain came tumbling out, "What's a skitter?"

Larry's grin grew a few millimeters. "Why, Colleen, I'd say you, but I'm afraid it'd make you blub."

He seemed really amused by this response, probably because I was now wondering what "blub" meant, although I thought I could parse out the meaning from the word. It sounded like a shortened version of "blubber," so it was either a fat joke or it had something to do with crying. I took it to be the latter and said, "Ah, so an insult. I can take it."

Larry's eyes lit up and he said, "Well, you're not numpty, that's something."

As odd as this meeting was, it was fast losing its mystical allure and was leaving me feeling irritated. I no longer felt like continuing it. I turned, not sure where I was going, but deciding that leaving was marginally better than staying.

Larry immediately said, "Wait, Mary-Claire! I'm sorry. It's a lot to take in at one time, no? A skitter is an annoying young person, which, if I may be forgiven, is exactly what you appeared to be when you were eying me gold, and numpty means stupid, which you're obviously not since you figured out what blub was referring to. I'll be laying off my Irish now, as I see that it's not terribly welcome at the moment. Friends?"

I turned back around and wiped the sweat off my brow as the salty beads were burning my eyes. So I wasn't leaving angry, but I still just wanted to get out of the blasted heat. "Sure, whatever, friends. So now what?"

Larry smiled and, with light hummingbird-like movements, was on my shoulder.

"Now I'll be going home with you."

~Chapter 3~

It took almost an hour to get home. I was really late, and I knew it. My brother, Mike, would already have been home alone for almost two hours, and if I couldn't calm him down, he would tell my mom for sure. I didn't want to deal with her anger and disappointment today. Even though I could feel the weight and warmth of Larry's small body on my shoulder as I walked home through the familiar streets, I wasn't entirely convinced that I hadn't imagined everything and that the heat on my shoulders wasn't emanating from a localized sunburn. In fact, he had been seemingly uncharacteristically quiet on our walk home, so I had begun to think it was indeed all a dream. After all, I wasn't lugging home a heavy pot of gold, the impossible rainbow no longer glittered in the sky like a demented party banner, and the rhythmic Irish voice was no longer insulting me in a language I wasn't quite sure was English.

I felt the pressure on my neck again and decided it was only my addled brain that made it feel heavy. So, I put my hand to it to feel if it was painful and got a muffled "Cop on, keep your hands to yourself!" I almost tripped in surprise. It couldn't be just a fantasy. And if it was, it was one that spoke in tongues.

"I wish you would just zap me home," I said as the sun beat down. I decided it was time to test this whole situation.

"Ha, lass! I told ya, only true wishes," Larry said. He sounded mostly disinterested.

"I'm pretty sure I truly wish for it," I said, feeling irritated. I truly wanted to get out of the hot sun, and I truly wanted to stop walking. I *truly* wanted to be home.

"Ah Mary-Claire, a true wish comes from so deep within you that you almost don't need to say it out loud. I can hear it in the beating of your heart. I can see it in the light in your eyes. I can feel it in the sound of your voice," he said softly, and although I had started discounting most of what he said as nonsense, I knew that this was true.

I found myself contemplating this new development. How would I know what a true wish was, and if I didn't know, how would he? And what if my true wishes were dark and shouldn't see the light of day? What then? Could I un-wish it? Could I have a do-over? This information brought me less comfort than I thought it would.

I finally neared our apartment complex and stopped to wait for the light to change. As I did so, I found myself wondering if I had waited for this light, or any light, stop sign, or obeyed any road signs in my insane trek. It was a weird thought, but from the fog of close memory and confusion, it seemed like now that I had heard more than a few car horns as I followed the impossible rainbow. I wondered how close I had come to being killed during my break from reality, and this musing kept me from noticing the changing of the light in front of me.

A rude push from behind and an angry "If you're not going to cross, get out of the way! Idiot!" made me realize that it was now safe to cross. I started to move forward when "Shut it, you right gowl!" came from the leprechaun seated on my shoulder in a surprisingly strong, definitely male, and accented voice. "Larry!" I hissed and shook my hair a little more violently than I would normally. I glanced behind me, and the guy who pushed me now looked confused and backed up a little. He shot me a worried glance, then gave me a wide berth as he entered the crosswalk.

I hurried across behind the guy and heard a chuckle in my ear. That tiny man persisted in being real, no matter how many times I told myself that it was impossible. I shook my head hard again, but this time it was to try and clear it. However, now I was rewarded with a sharp tug on one red curl.

"Aye there, girl! Quit that! You're going to knock me clean off!"

We had finally reached the apartment complex. I looked around at the cracked and dirty white stucco. Well, white was the original intent; now, it was the color of unbrushed teeth. All of the condos looked the same, two-story, a door front and center, with a large arched window to the left and a small window and sliding glass door to the right. Curving out in front of the sliding door was an arched reddish cinder block retaining wall, about four feet high, with a small patio. We had a forest green metal bistro set on ours, which looked really cute, but branded your thighs if you had the audacity to sit on it during the day. Other tenants had plastic chairs and tables, which were slightly more useful, but my mom saw everything with a realtor's eyes. Right after the first three tenants of reality, location, location, location, came my mom's fourth, staging. A red tile roof hung over the small covered portico above the door, something which was probably supposed to add a point of interest but just seemed out of place and tacked on. There were two windows on the second floor and a large window/door with a juliet balcony with a black wrought iron railing on the right. Again, probably supposed to be a cool architectural detail, but really just highlighted the drabness of the entire facade. Plus, with four on one building front, it looked like a copy-and-paste of bad Photoshop. I sighed and walked to condo #3278. If it weren't for the white numbers on turquoise and burnt orange tiles, I'd probably have trouble finding my own apartment.

I put my key in the lock and then realized Mike hadn't bothered to lock it when he came home. I winced and looked around the parking lot for my mom's car; I prayed it wasn't there. If she had come home and found Mike alone and the door unlocked, no leprechaun in the world was going to save me from what was to come. My first true wish would have been to save my life. Although, did I want to save the current life I was living? I shook my head and half laughed. Man, having found a leprechaun had made me somewhat dramatic. Fortunately, I didn't see her car, so I focused on the task at hand.

"Mike," I said as I entered the gloriously artificially cool apartment; it felt great after the prolonged heat I had experienced today. I soaked the cold in through every pore of my body. I breathed in deeply and then called for my brother again and again. And then I frowned.

There was no answer, and the apartment was strangely quiet. I expected the TV or a video game or something. There was nothing, and I began to worry. I think the events of the day had taken their toll on me because instead of being afraid that someone had taken my brother, I had an irrational fear that some*thing* had slid into our world on the rainbow with Larry. I didn't know what mythical creatures leprechauns hung out with, but I imagined there must be some other ones, and not all of them could be nice. While Larry had been seducing me with the promise of wishes, had another Irish legend come and taken Mike, like a mummy? Wait, were there Irish mummies? I doubted it. They'd rot rather than desiccate. Was there an Irish monster? Was this the most important mental conversation I could be having right now?

I looked around the apartment quickly, checking for signs of intrusion. The white ceramic tiled floor in the entryway was clean, well as clean as I had left it this morning. I mean, it's white tile, it only gets, and stays, so clean. But there were no bloody drag marks, at least. I walked through the small arched doorway into the kitchen on the right. The kitchen table sat undisturbed in the breakfast nook, and the countertops were clear of clutter and any sign of struggle. I checked the sliding glass door onto the small side patio, making sure it was locked before I decided nothing was amiss in the kitchen.

I walked out of the kitchen and went to the laundry room behind the kitchen. It was small, and I could see the entire area. I glanced out the tiny window in the back of the room which looked out on the courtyard between buildings in the back. There was no one walking between buildings, and the desolation of the courtyard only enhanced my feeling of unease.

I walked quickly across to the bathroom on the right. It was small, with a pedestal sink, toilet, and a tiny shower, not enough room to turn around, but big enough, so the condo was listed as two full baths. It was lit from the outside with a rectangular opaque glass block window that took up nearly half the wall of the shower. This was the feature of the apartment that I enjoyed the most. Like its counterpart in the upstairs bathroom, it allowed a great deal of light in and was decorative without looking random. This bathroom was Mike's; my mother and I both agreed that we'd rather share with each other than with him, so it wasn't exactly clean, but I doubted anything was hiding in the clutter. Still, I nudged a mound of towels on the floor with my toe. And then I stomped on it for good measure. Nothing squished out, which I took as a good sign. Also, as I looked at the pile of at least ten towels, I realized my brother had access to too many towels. I stepped out of the room and into the hallway.

"MIKE!" I said, this time loud enough that I'm sure the neighbors heard. Again, I was met with silence, except for a chuckle by my ear. I flicked at Larry as I walked through the entryway toward the living room. I glanced quickly up the white carpeted stairs to where the bedrooms lay. I'd check there if I didn't find him in front of the TV, but the top of the stairs looked dark and forbidding, we kept the blinds in all the bedrooms closed in a desperate attempt to keep the heat at bay, and I was not-so-bravely going to check all the brightly lit areas before heading into the gloom.

The entry into the living room was less a doorway and more an open room with a wide-arched walkway. I could see the back of the green upholstered sofa and it was in the same position as when I left this morning, as were the cream-colored overstuffed chair to the left of it and the cracking maroon vinyl bean bag chair to the right. The coffee table was positioned at an odd interval between the couch and the TV, which might mean something had disturbed it, but most likely meant that Mike had roughly pushed it when he got off the couch at some point. I honestly only noted it because it wasn't staged properly, and thanks to my mother, I noticed stuff like that. Not seeing anything of immediate interest, I reluctantly backed out of the room and was about to head upstairs when I heard footsteps on the tile behind me.

I spun around in fear and saw Mike come around the corner of the couch, his dark head bent over his video game and earbuds in his ears.

"WHAT!" he said, mimicking my shout and not even looking up from his game. For some reason, with all the thoughts running through my brain and my uncontrolled terror at the thought of losing him, his lackadaisical attitude angered me.

I could hear the frantic whoosh of blood coursing through my ears and felt my heart trying to escape my chest. Calm down Mary-Claire, I told myself. Calm down, or you'll have to explain yourself, and he's smarter than he looks. I glanced at his empty face, his eyes trying to simultaneously look at me and his games. He failed at both and grimaced when whatever character he was playing died. I held back a smile; he'd almost have to be smarter than he looked, or he wouldn't be able to walk and chew gum.

"You forgot to lock the door, dummy," I said, grabbed the system from his hands, yanked the earbuds out as I did so, and forced him to acknowledge me. He looked up, all the anger of an eleven-year-old in his blue eyes, but I think he saw the fear, or terror even, in mine, because his demeanor changed immediately, and he got defiant.

"So what? You were supposed to be right behind me."

"It's Tuesday, I'm never 'right behind' you on Tuesdays."

My argument must have satisfied him, or at least confused him, because he took another U-turn in attitude--straight to whiny. "I'm huuuunnngry," he said and reached for his game.

"Oh, seriously! You know where the snacks are, stop being so lazy!" I stalked through the entryway and into the kitchen. He followed me like a puppy, with a pleading and expectant look on his face at the mention of food. I went to the corner pantry, opened the door, and tossed several baggies of snacks on the counter. He looked at the less-than-nutritious array on the counter and smiled at me. My mother would like to think that I would make him a personal charcuterie board after school, but she'd be lucky if I opened a can of mandarin oranges for him most days. He grabbed three, and I took two out of his hands as he passed and gave him back his game.

"Did you do your homework?"

"Mmmmffth," he said, having already deposited himself back on the couch in the family room, stuffed his face, and commenced killing a Lego creature or winning Mario Kart.

I sighed, cleaned up the snacks, and looked gratefully around the kitchen. She wasn't home; I wasn't *that* late. Mike was now sated, and I knew that another hour of video gaming would help him forget that I didn't come home when he thought I should. I knew that, at eleven, he could technically tell time on a clock, but my brother wasn't big on details. He just knew that after however long of playing games, he was hungry. The homework issue would have to be dealt with at another time. I didn't want to disturb him and rile up his memory for my mother.

"Are you always so off your nut?" an Irish brogue breathed in my ear.

"What?!? No," I said, gritting my teeth. I had truly lost it, and I did not want Larry the Leprechaun to know what I had been thinking. "It's just little brothers."

"Do you want me to turn him into a dog?"

"What? Can you really, what?! No," I said, shocked and confused. Had I wished that silently? Did that desire well up from my heart? Could he actually read my thoughts? Wow, things could turn ugly really quickly, and my three wishes were going to be the stuff of horror movies and "The Twilight Zone."

Larry chuckled. "No, Colleen, I cannot alter the physical state of things. Rule Number One. So, I cannot take your brother and make him something more palatable."

I smiled. I loved Mike; he had been nice to have around during the divorce and on nights when Mom had extra-late appointments, but sometimes, a dog did sound better. A dog would have greeted me with sloppy wet kisses and hyperactive joy. And then still probably whined for a snack. So not much different than a brother, and I was definitely OK with not getting the sloppy kisses today.

"So, rule number one, no dog, got it," I said, distracted. I sat down on the cheap wicker and steel bar stool at the kitchen counter, which looked good, but wasn't the most comfortable, and focused more on opening my backpack and getting my homework than what the mythical creature was saying.

"No, Mary-Claire, Rule Number One is I cannot alter the physical state of things," Larry said, sounding so serious that I looked up from the algebra I had been willing myself to want to do.

"Lighten up, it was a joke. Don't be," I began, and scrunched up my face searching for the word, "...numpty?" Larry didn't even crack a smile, which I thought was odd.

"No, you need to understand," he said, clambering up on my textbook and planting his miniature body directly in my view; it made math impossible so that all I could do was concentrate totally on him. "I cannot make someone who is sick healthy; that would be altering their physical state. I cannot make your body different, your hair a different color, or your eyes. I cannot make this apartment bigger or your brother smaller. I *cannot* alter the *physical* state of things."

He looked really serious, so I tried to focus, but too much had already happened today, and my brain was reeling. I needed to get my homework done, I needed to start something simple for dinner, and I needed to just wrap my head around that I now had a leprechaun companion for the next little while. I had the feeling, though, that he wanted to make sure I understood exactly what he was saying, so I looked intently into his eyes and said, "I understand, Larry, and I won't wish for anything like that." Then I looked past him to the numbers and letters on the page. If he couldn't make me magically smarter, then I needed to do my homework.

The newly familiar smile turned to a frown, and his eyes gleamed. "Oh, you will, Mary-Claire. You will wish for that; they all do. But I'll be just warning you now: I cannot do it."

With that, he hopped off the book and seemed to disappear entirely. Great, now that I was interested, he left! What the heck did that mean? Were these little knowledge bombs something he was going to keep doing? How would I know when they were important versus when it was Larry just talking? I chewed my lip and looked around for a moment, wondering what I should do. Should I chase after him and learn more? But in the end, I voted for practical over the magical creature treasure hunt. I opened my book with a sigh and got to work.

~Chapter 4~

My mom came home just after I had fried some chicken, made mashed potatoes, and finished my math homework. Actually, I was shocked at what I managed to accomplish. It must've been at least two hours since I got home from my unlikely adventure. And since she had run so late, I had even managed to pull Mike off the video game and make him finish his homework. Not bad for a really strange afternoon.

And I did it all myself because my good-for-nothing-so-far leprechaun had not helped in the slightest, even after he had suddenly reappeared in the middle of peeling potatoes. Not even when I said, "I wish for some help with dinner." He had merely smiled and said, "Three true wishes, and I'll be knowing the difference." I wasn't totally sure he understood his own rules because I was pretty sure at that moment I did want help with dinner.

Mom opened the door, dropped her laptop bag carefully onto the floor, walked into the kitchen, sniffed the air, and smiled. She had the same red hair I had, although it was straight, and age was apparently going to fade the brilliance a little. Her face looked young, but stress was beginning to lightly line it. I got my dad's eyes, but sometimes I wish I had her deep blue ones. They were arresting, even when they were sad and tired, like tonight. She was slender, more so than when my parents divorced. She had stopped eating for a while, and even now, her appetite was barely coming back. She wore flowy light blue linen pants and a silky sleeveless white top. She was always picture-perfect, except for her shoes. My mother was fashionable to a point; it was her shoes that she refused to compromise on. She wore sneakers to work. She tried in the beginning to wear heels, but hours of walking people through house after house had shown her the impracticality of that. But comfort didn't necessarily mean a total lack of fashion; she had sneakers in every color of the rainbow, and the ones that peeped out under the linen pants were the exact same color ice blue. They always either matched her pants or her shirt.

"I had hoped you would start dinner," she said, and she came up, tucked a ringlet behind my ear, and kissed my cheek. "Thank you, sweetie, it was a rough day."

"You're home later than I thought you would be," I said, keeping my voice as light as possible, hoping I didn't sound petulant. I really wasn't upset. With how late an arrival I had made, the extra time meant that I had taken care of everything I needed to do. But more to the point, the interval had given me a nice distraction from thinking about Larry. This became a necessity because he had seemed a bit concerned with my cooking skills once the water boiled hard and splashed into the hot oil, causing a few mini explosions. I may have sprinkled a few drops of water into the oil after that, making him jump, and, finally, he pulled his vanishing act as I finished. He had yet to return.

"I know, I'm really sorry. We had a husband and wife walk in at four who wanted to go look at houses this afternoon. Only Greg and I were there, and he had to take his kid to the doctor or something. Anyway, I didn't really have to fight for it, but then I had to do the work."

I started plating up dinner. "It's ok, don't worry about it. Did you get the sale?"

"Well, they didn't buy anything tonight, but there were two houses they liked, and they have a few more they want to look at tomorrow. I think it's promising." She smiled brightly, but there was exhaustion behind it. I hoped they would buy something tomorrow.

"Then it was worth it," I said as I placed the plates on the table. No matter how many times I've done this since Dad left, every time I place three plates on the four-person table, I always get sad. The empty chair is a solid reminder of what used to be. There were only three bar stools at the counter, so I liked to set dinner there. But somehow, tonight, it felt better to set the actual table. The wicker and metal barstools were new, something we bought out of necessity for our new apartment. The table was solid oak from our days of living as a two-income/two-parent family and much nicer. And tonight, I wanted nicer.

Mom took in the fully set table, pausing to look somewhat pointedly at the counter, and then looked at me a little oddly.

"Honey, I'm not complaining, as this is really nice, but why are you in such a good mood? Did something great happen at school today?"

The question caught me off guard, and I sloshed the milk I was pouring for Mike over the side of the glass. I gained a little time by sponging up the mess, and then looked at my mom and said totally honestly, "No, nothing special happened at school. I just understood my algebra today, so maybe that's why."

Mom seemed somewhat unconvinced, but just then, Mike wandered in, and she took the handheld game out of his hands and made him hug her. This interruption gave me time to finish placing the food and drinks around the table. As I put the Kelly-green napkins by the plates, I remembered Larry and looked around. It occurred to me that I hadn't seen him for an hour. As I glanced at the counter, I saw a swish of green dart behind a canister in the corner.

I was going to get the saltshaker from the corner cabinet when I found him behind the canister, smiling to himself.

"Do you need dinner?" I asked quietly. I was trying to keep my family from committing me against my will, but I also thought this would be the polite thing to do. Or would it? Did he eat normal food? Could he? Maybe he only ate ambrosia and drank the nectar of the gods. No, wait, that's Greek mythology. Red-capped mushrooms and fairy-tear spring water, then?

"No, I'll be getting my own later; thank you, Colleen. I'm just enjoying getting to know your family. Now don't spend too much time talking to me, or they'll think you're off your nut!"

I walked back to the table, but my mind was occupied again. What was I going to do with Larry? Where would he sleep? What was he going to eat? Would he be with me at all times, and did that include the bathroom? Now I was feeling sick to my stomach.

"Mary-Claire, I asked how French Club was." My mom's voice cut through my questions, and I looked up to find myself eating. French Club? Was that really what I had been doing this afternoon before it all started? It was hard to think back that long ago.

"Fine," I said strategically through a mouthful of chicken, and, as I suspected, I got a fifteen-minute lecture on table manners, which freed me to clear my mind and remember my day. Mike cut in at the end of the lecture to tell my mom some exciting news about an elementary school chess club or something, which gave me more time.

"So, Mary-Claire, Mike's hogged most of dinner; why don't you tell me something about your day other than understanding algebra," she smiled as she said it, so I guess my good mood was catching.

I had had plenty of time to think, so I was prepared to give an answer this time. "Mrs. Montoya said my essay was particularly well thought out and reasoned, so that's something."

I hoped that would put her off the scent, but mothers don't seem to be as easily distracted as eleven-year-old boys. "Honey, I was hoping to hear something along the social lines. We've been here almost six months, and I still never hear you talk about friends or..." She was trailing off on her own when Mike interrupted, "I have tons of friends. And I think I have a girlfriend. At least Sasha told me she was my girlfriend," he said, looking confused. "I don't actually remember agreeing to it."

Mom laughed, and I joined in. While I didn't need the reminder that my brother was more socially adept than I was, it was nice of him to keep taking the pressure off me, no matter if it was on purpose or not. Except, it didn't really seem to take the pressure off. As we smiled at each other over Mike's head, Mom got a questioning look in her eye. I frowned and shook my head, and that seemed to do the trick. Giving me her best honey-I-understand look, Mom smiled once more and cleared her throat to catch Mike's attention.

"It was so nice of you to make dinner, Mary-Claire. I'll do the dishes," my mom said. Her throat clearing didn't do the job, however, because Mike's head remained bent over his plate. Apparently, the girlfriend thing took up most of his brain power. She shook her head, got up, and started clearing the table. On a different day, in a different mood, I might have offered to help just for some extra time with her, but not tonight.

"Thanks, Mom, I've got to study for a biology quiz," I said, grabbing my backpack off the kitchen counter. Just before I got there, I had seen a streak of green race from the canisters to the open pack. So, I guessed I'd have company while I studied. I found the thought even less appealing than normal–odd how quickly having a leprechaun companion had become *normal*– because of my previous bathroom musings than I would have before. Was I going to have his companionship in there as well?

My mom smiled at me and nudged Mike's chair with her foot. He looked up quickly, and she gave him a look that said, "Help me now." Mike, with just a show of complaining, got up to help. I was very grateful for that. I knew my mom was tired, but I just couldn't do it tonight.

I walked out of the kitchen, slinging my backpack over my shoulder. "Your family is nice," a voice said from the depths of my backpack. I paused in the hallway right out of the kitchen, set my backpack on the floor, and opened it, all the while making a play at rummaging through it, and lifted him out and onto my shoulder. I glanced quickly at the kitchen to make sure neither of them saw me; I needn't have bothered with the play-acting. My mother and brother were deep in discussion about his girlfriend problem.

"Thank you," I said as I walked up the stairs. Although it had only been a few hours, I was getting oddly used to the feeling of something living tucked under my hair.

"No father?" he asked as I walked into my room.

I stopped walking and looked straight ahead, wishing this conversation was over now. "No, well, I mean, he exists, of course, but not with us anymore."

I expected more questions, but Larry stayed silent after that. He stayed silent through most of my studying, too—a silent living statue watching everything I did. Not creepy, not creepy at all. I had a difficult time concentrating, which naturally made studying difficult.

"I can't make you smarter," he said just after I had sighed in frustration over not remembering a phylum. I jumped slightly and looked up at him with a sharp retort on my tongue, but I saw his smile and realized he was just teasing me. I turned briefly back to my textbook, but it was even more useless now that he was talking to me. I flipped the book closed and looked expectantly at Larry.

"Do you want to give me more rules?"

"No, you're not even trying to wish, so it seems pointless," he said. Then looking directly into my eyes, he said, "I just need you to understand I'm here until you wish three true wishes."

I stared back at him and said, "OK, you're making a big deal about these 'true' wishes, do you want to explain that?"

Larry sighed and looked out the window where the harsh metallic blue of the afternoon sky had finally given way to the more soothing pink-gray of dusk. "Ah, Colleen, if I have to explain, it will do no good. I'll be knowin' when what you wish for is what you really want."

"My name is Mary-Claire, *Larry*," I said. I was irritated that he didn't seem to remember my name.

"Gah, you Americans! It just means girlie. Better, *Mary-Claire*?*"

I scowled, "Sure, that you'll explain, but not a 'true' wish?"

"No, as I said before, Colleen, I'll be knowin' when ya truly wished," Larry said, and he laughed lightly, pleased with himself.

I sighed in frustration. How was he supposed to know what I truly wished for if I didn't know myself? I thought I might have truly wished for help this afternoon, but apparently, I was kidding myself. I knew I wished for my father to be back home, but in order for me to truly want that, there would have to be no half-brother or sister on the way. And since Larry couldn't change the physical aspect of things, that couldn't happen.

I stared at the closed textbook and *truly* wished him away, and when I looked up, he was gone. I searched under the desk and bed and in my closet and found nothing. Even though he had done this twice so far today, I was confused by this turn of events. He had seemed in the middle of a wish lecture. Could I have possibly wished him away? I looked around once more but still found nothing. Strange. Well, was it strange? I mean, I was looking for a leprechaun, for crying out loud. How could I possibly call *not* finding one strange?

"Larry," I said quietly. I hadn't looked at a clock in a while, and I had no idea what time it was. I couldn't be sure Mike or my mom weren't already upstairs, and I'm pretty sure calling out a male name in my bedroom would be cause for alarm—although they would be more alarmed if they knew what kind of male it was.

"*Larry,*" I whisper-hissed one more time. Nothing.

I shook my head and smiled. Suddenly a much more palatable idea took hold in my brain: I had been hallucinating all afternoon. Funny how that was the more comforting of the two warring options. I might have nearly had sunstroke, but there wasn't a leprechaun running around Phoenix spouting nonsense about wishes. I could have been close to death, but it made me feel infinitely better to believe that version of reality. I got back to my studies and even went to sleep at what my mom would term a reasonable hour.

~Chapter 5~

I got up the next morning and quietly and quickly searched my room. After finding nothing, I realized the distinct possibility that I had dreamed most of what I "remembered" about yesterday. It seemed a lot more plausible than that I had hallucinated following a rainbow to its end and finding a leprechaun lounging against a pot of gold sitting at its termination. And it was certainly more plausible than it had actually happened, and said leprechaun was now at my beck and call. Still, before I went to the bathroom to take my shower, I looked carefully once more around my room for the little man. He was nowhere to be found.

Smiling at the insanity of it, I grabbed my towel and school clothes and ran to the bathroom. I had to get in before my stinky preteen brother managed to get out of bed. I took a long, hot shower and was bothered by a slight sunburn on my arms and face. I got out of the shower, wiped the steam off the mirror, and examined myself in it. Red hair, limp and curly from the water, green eyes, and, oh yes, a sunburn across my nose and cheeks and definitely on my arms.

I frowned at the soggy reflection. I did not have a sunburn yesterday morning, and I couldn't remember anything real I had done yesterday to cause a burn. I was now fully convinced that the whole "Larry" was, in fact, a sunstroke dream. I knew there was no way I had walked miles on a September afternoon with the sun beating down. In fact, due to my stupidly fair coloring, I religiously avoided the Arizona sun most days. I was a big believer in sunscreen, hats, and the great indoors, all in an effort to avoid skin cancer and premature aging, the latter being more pressing than the former in my teenage mind. Actually, truthfully, those were my mom's worries. I just hated sunburns, which brought me back to my present situation.

I slathered on some aloe and frowned again at the mirror. This time not for the sunburn but for the general reflection I saw therein. I've been told that people are really envious of natural red hair, curly red hair to boot, but I've never met them. I mean, I know I'm not ugly or anything, and I love my green eyes. And sometimes, on a good day, I love my hair. Heck, I could even admit that someday I'll probably appreciate my Irish heritage, but not now, not today. Not when Sean is mooning over the tanned beauty of Tessa.

I got dressed and returned to my room to make my bed and straighten up before going downstairs. My mom was a real stickler for that sort of thing. Once, years ago, in another life, when I still had a dad, she came and got me out of school to come back and clean my room and make my bed. Even though I was ninety-nine percent positive that she wouldn't have the time now to do so, the memory haunted me every morning. Admittedly, though, I didn't fear her giving it the army go-over. This morning, with all of my mirror musings, it was a pretty dismal attempt. I tugged at a corner of the turquoise bedspread, frowned when that fix seemed to cause more wrinkles, and threw the pillows at the mess. I stepped back and surveyed the overall mess. I shrugged to myself. At least all the bedding was off the floor.

"Good morning, Colleen," a voice came from behind me, at ear level. I whirled around and saw Larry perched on my dresser, leaning against my jewelry box. He was twirling around his arm the turquoise ring my father had bought me when we first moved to Arizona ten years ago. We had left the green leaves and salt air of Boston for the cacti and dust of Phoenix, and I was sad and angry. The first night we spent in our new southwestern home, my dad had brought home this beautiful stone, the color of the Caribbean Sea he told me. The blue of the stone against the purity of the silver had mesmerized me and dried my tears. Of all the things I had misplaced in the last ten years, I had never lost that ring. I couldn't wear it anymore; it was ridiculously small on me but seeing it in the grasp of my supposed vision jerked me back to a reality I wasn't sure I wanted.

I gaped at him, and he smiled back. Had it been *real*? My mind reeled like it had yesterday afternoon, which brought back instant, unwelcome, and *real* memories of yesterday afternoon. I *had* walked miles like a moron, I *had* found the childhood dream, and I *had* indeed gotten myself a tiny green-clad companion. Not knowing what else to do, I snatched the ring from him, tossed it angrily back into the jewelry box, and slammed the metal lid shut. I didn't care that I didn't like my father anymore; I cared that a stupid mythical creature was going to lose the only thing I had left of him that was all mine.

"OK, got it. Don't touch the ring. You could have just told me," he said, his voice genial, but there was an undertone of ice, absurdly like I had managed to hurt his feelings, if he even had those.

"Oh sure, just like you tell me all the rules up front too. More fun for me," I said, attempting to mimic his Irish brogue in the last sentence. It was an odd, miserable failure, so I went immediately to more pressing questions. "Where did you disappear last night, and where were you this morning?" I asked. I didn't add, "because I was really happy when I thought you were just my crazy imagination." He could find that rude.

"Last night, you seemed preoccupied. I thought you might want some time to digest current events, so I took myself on a tour of your gaff. It's larger than I expected, and what with dodging your ma and brother, I got back a wee bit later than I expected. You seemed knackered, so I just made meself a bed. And in the morning, well, I know that teenage girls like to get themselves ready, and I know they like their privacy, so I left." I sensed a small bit of disdain there and bristled, even though some of the words left me wondering what the heck he was trying to say.

"What," I said, "You don't like privacy?"

"O' course I do, but you humans act like it'd be the end of the world if I saw you naked. I don't know why you flatter yourself; you're far too big and gangly for me."

My offense must have shown on my face because he hastily added, "Not just you, Mary-Claire. All humans are large and unwieldy when you're my height."

I nodded slightly, relieved that at least the bathroom question was answered. I picked up my backpack from the floor and, in a conciliatory gesture, held it open at the dresser height for him to climb in. This morning had not gotten off to a great start, and I suspected my joy at the whole thing not being real and subsequent depression when that idea was shattered had something to do with this.

"Did you get something for breakfast?" I asked as I left my room and started down the hallway to the stairs. In a few minutes, I wouldn't be able to talk to him anymore, but I wanted to make sure.

"Oh, Colleen, you are a kind one, first impressions notwithstanding. Yes, I did. Your ma went back to her room as I got to the kitchen and your brother came in as I was leaving. He's not observant, that one. And not careful either. I almost got stepped on."

I smiled. "Yeah, normally, he's always on the lookout for leprechauns, but I guess today was an off day."

Larry smiled back and then tucked himself down in the depths of the backpack.

Mike was eating a mixing bowl of cereal when I came into the kitchen. He looked up when I came and said through a mouthful of soggy Lucky Charms, "Mom said to tell you she's going to try to be home early today. So, you better not be late again." Then he went back to eating his cereal and playing his game.

I stared at the top of his head and wondered what went on in that tiny brain. I had assumed he had forgotten about coming home to an empty house yesterday. He hadn't ratted me out to Mom, which I hadn't known if I should attribute to him forgetting or actually being nice. We're not as close as we were right after Dad left, but I guess there's still some of that camaraderie left. I rumpled his hair and whispered in his ear, "Thanks, little dude. I'll make you a special snack when I get home today. Quesadilla?"

He looked up from his game, and I got a happy, slobbery nod for my trouble. I hummed as I poured my own normal-sized bowl of cereal. Well, the morning had been off to a rocky start, but it had definitely gotten better. I didn't think Larry could exactly take the credit, but I gave it to him anyway. It made me feel more inclined toward him, and since we were going to be bunkmates for a while, I wanted it to be on good terms.

Mike got on the bus okay, but I was deliberately late getting ready. I was just finishing slowly placing all my books and papers in my backpack when I heard the whine of the bus engine leaving my stop. My goal was accomplished, but I had missed one small detail. Just as the engines roared into full throttle, my mother came hopping out of her room, one shoe on one foot and the other seemingly protesting going on the other.

"Mary-Claire, honestly! You know I don't have time to drop you off at school. I have a showing in twenty..." She glanced down at her watch and then grabbed her briefcase and keys and shoved her foot Cinderella-stepsister style into the stubborn shoe. "Oh crap, fifteen minutes! Have a good day."

This last sentence was flung behind her like a just-discovered sock that had been linted to her blouse. I knew my mom loved me, but some days it was easier to believe it than others.

"Love you too," I shouted at the door, just in case she could hear, but as I finished the words, I heard the creak of her car door as she opened it. She'd been in a minor accident with the pillar in our parking spot out front one too many times, and the driver's side door protested opening every time now. The sound is usually oddly comforting because it always told me when she was home. This morning it sounded melancholy to me. Like I was being left on my own to battle whatever supernatural forces lurked around the corners. I shook my head vigorously to hopefully clear it. This was actually what I had wanted. I could easily walk to school on time, I was the first of many bus stops on the way to school, and I needed some alone time with Larry. I had to know what was expected of me in this deal.

He stayed in the backpack through most of the parking lot. It was a bit busy here and loud with all the tenants leaving for various errands, appointments, and, of course, jobs. But once we were well on our way, he hopped onto his normal place on my shoulder.

"Lovely morning, lassie, don't you think?" he said. "I just love the sunshine here. Don't you?"

"Yeah, beautiful," I said distractedly, then I looked at Larry. He was wearing the same outfit from yesterday, except now he was wearing a ridiculous green sun visor with a black band and the same stupidly large gold buckle. I started for a moment but then continued, "Do I get any more rules today?"

"Oh, rules, ha! You humans seem to think they're so important. They're not, really. I mean, they're of no concern to you until they are. However, there is one, though, that I must tell you about now; you can't tell anyone else about me."

"Like I want anyone to know," I said, snorting. Since I didn't believe he would appear to someone on my command, I sincerely doubted I would be fool enough to tell someone I had a leprechaun consort.

"Oh, you say that, but some people feel the need to let others know about their good fortune."

"Oh, so some people think of this as good fortune. Nice to know," I said. I realized it sounded pretty harsh, and I didn't know if leprechauns picked up on sarcasm. "Sorry, just kidding. I promise I won't tell anyone. Anything else?"

Larry chortled. "You might not think so now, but you will. When you finally start your wishing, let me see, what's another rule I can give you? Oh, right. You can't wish for more wishes. That's an old rule, I suppose. Did you already know that one?"

I smiled, "It's the first rule given by every genie, so I guessed as much."

This time it was Larry's turn to snort, "Dense djinns. Their magic is so much fluff and mirrors. Either you're magic, or you're not. And if you are, then you should have enough power to get yourself out of a bottle."

I found myself smiling. So, there's rivalry in the magical world. And the next thought I had was: *genies are real*? Larry saw my confusion and seemingly read my mind, "Oh yes, djinns are as real as I am."

Weird how much sense that sentence made. Genies are as real as leprechauns. For most of the world, that would mean that they existed only in stories, movies, and children's imaginations. Yet for me, it meant that a whole new magical dimension had just opened. So leprechauns and genies exist. Check. I wondered what other fairy tale creatures would turn out to inhabit the preternatural part of our world.

"So, do you know any genies?" I asked, wanting to keep the conversation going. I forgot how long the walk to school felt in the mornings, and I doubted he would appreciate me putting in my earbuds.

"First things first, they're called djinns. The term 'genie' is very derogatory. So, in the future, please refrain." He seemed so serious that I was instantly chastened. Feeling like a small child, I meekly said, "I'm sorry. I truly didn't know."

He sounded forgiving as he said, "It's grand. I was only coddin you."

Okay…whatever that meant. But he sounded happy, so I took it as a good sign. Larry started in again, "Oh yeah, I knew a chancer of a djinn. He was the kind that would steal the blessings from the Holy Water. Oh, we had fun!"

He chuckled in my ear, but I tried to work out what he was saying. I was still on "coddin" and now "chancer." And then something else he had said earwormed its way into my consciousness. "What? Can you actually *steal* the blessings from Holy Water?"

Larry snickered, "Oh right, you don't speak Irish. He wasn't the best sort of being. Always getting into trouble and using his magic for mischief. Oh, didn't he love to mess with humans, maybe more than meself! I miss the lad." His voice got wistful towards the end.

I actually felt sorry for Larry. "Did he die?" I said softly, almost reverently.

There was a moment of silence and then a loud snort in my ear. It hurt—not a lot, but still.

"What part of *immortality* does your human head have trouble with? I guess we don't all live forever, but goodness, I've seen this world before your kind took over. Honestly, dead?! She thinks he's dead!" I could feel his body shaking as he laughed silently on my shoulder. He finally took in a huge gasp of air, and this time I could hear him. Apparently, human stupidity is a real gag to the fabled.

"Well then, what the heck happened to him? Why do you miss him?" I asked, thoroughly confused and nearing school. I had to get this settled before djinns, chancers, and wishes took over my head.

"The eejit got himself stuck in a bottle, he did. Messed with the wrong human and got sucked right in. Oh, he was cheesed off! His wee face as he looked out from the glass." Instead of sounding sad, Larry was having trouble speaking through his laughter. "Oh, he was hopping! He wanted me to use me magic to get him out, but I'm not wasting me powers on a creature so foolish he gets stuck behind glass. I did conjure him a lovely divan. And I sent him a lovely bunch of flowers…in a replica of the bottle he's trapped in! Oh, that got him!"

He was laughing so hard he seemed to be wobbling on my shoulder. It seemed particularly cruel of him, so I innocently said, "Yes, a backpack is much roomier."

The laughter stopped for a minute, but then, to my surprise, he chuckled once more. "Quite right Mary-Claire. Quite right." And with that, we arrived on the school campus, and I felt him scramble to climb back in.

~Chapter 6~

"Okay, Colleen," Larry said from his perch just inside my pack. "What's the craic?"

I stumbled into the guy in front of me. Walking and translating leprechaun were not easy. The kid looked back at me, and I gave him a small shrug. I've always wished there was a gesture for my bad. As he moved off, I mumbled to Larry, "What's the what?" I wasn't sure he heard or understood because I was trying to move my mouth as little as possible. Ventriloquism wasn't my forte.

The stumble and the shrug pushed some of the hair forward, and I felt Larry once again cop a squat on my shoulder. He chuckled in my ear. "I'm going to have to move closer if you're going to mumble instead of speak. I'll put it in words you understand, what's the coffee?"

I was more confused than ever. "The what?!" I asked louder than I meant. Brenna Tyson looked at me oddly as she passed and said, "They just announced the next assembly." I nodded in her direction as I realized the morning announcements were happening. I always hated that background noise during the din of morning hallway traffic, but today I guess it saved me. As if reading my face, she nodded back, said, "I wish they would wait until we're in class," and disappeared into the crowd.

Larry was kind enough to wait for her to pass before stage whispering, "I was asking what's the gossip? The who, what, when, where, and why of your social life. Who're the most likely candidates to get these wishes underway?"

I smiled but luckily avoided laughing out loud and looking crazy. "Oh, the *tea!*"

Larry giggled to himself, "The tea! Oh, I so love learning new words!"

I looked around at the hustle and bustle of teenagers running this way and that, trying to make sure to get to class on time or find the right person and be seen by the right person. *Most likely candidates?* I thought about that for just a minute before I realized I had no major players in my life other than my mom and brother. That thought, surrounded as I was by people who would enter the school and find "major players" in every class and every hallway, was more than depressing; it was disturbing. I walked through the throng of rowdy teens, watching them greet each other and talk of the day to come, and knew no one was seeking me.

"Um, well..." I said, hesitating for more time. I was just positive that Larry was the most popular leprechaun in the sky, and I didn't need his derision right now. I looked desperately around the crowded hallway. Surely there would be a person whose name I knew, a face I recognized, someone vaguely familiar. But the longer I looked, the lonelier I became in the crowd. I felt ridiculous in my quest, but I silently prayed that he assumed I was looking for someone specific and not simply *anyone* who might act as a friendly body.

Then to add to my abject humiliation, I heard in a soft tone, "Oh Mary-Claire, has it been so very hard?"

I fought back the dumb tears fighting their way out. Ok, so this most recent move hadn't been as stellar as I had hoped. Six months ago, after the divorce, we had sold our standard ranch home and moved into the apartment, and I had finished last year with about six weeks left in this new school. I told myself – and my mom when she had pushed the issue all last summer -- that it hadn't been enough time to make friends. This current school year was again only six weeks in, and I still felt as alone as I had on the last day of school a few months earlier. Still, not enough time to make friends, I repeated to myself. And while I was sure I would be just a dream to know under normal circumstances, apparently, depression wasn't the ice breaker I thought it would be.

"Dear, I think I know one wish I would make," Larry said softly.

For more friends, any *friends*? I didn't think that would be a wish that would work. What was he going to do, cast a spell on the entire school, making them find me irresistible?

"I'm doing fine," I said crossly, looking around for someone, *any*one I could introduce to him. I was breaking school rules and crossing the grass instead of the sidewalks to quickly get into the building. Maybe in there, I would find one face that wouldn't look blankly back at me when they had mistakenly made eye contact.

Then I saw Sean. He was standing at the main entrance to the school, leaning casually on the brick half-wall behind him. Sunlight played through his hair, highlighting the golden strands and lighting the red highlights on fire, and even from far away, I could see the deep blue of his eyes. His face was angular, masculine and so handsome.

"There," I said, hoping my voice sounded calm. "That's Sean. We've had some classes together."

Larry, tucked neatly into the curls on my shoulder, followed my gaze to the building. "Oh, Colleen, he's a right-looking Bob!"

I wrinkled my forehead, "Bob? His name is Sean."

"I just meant he was good-looking, honestly, ya eejit! I can hear and understand names well enough."

I found the word amusing, and it distracted both him and me enough that I wasn't caught staring longingly at Sean. In the movies, those shots are always the height of romance, but in real life, I was pretty sure I would give off more of a stalker vibe. This break also got Larry looking around for other potential friends. I was grateful. Sean and I weren't exactly best buddies, and I didn't want to field questions from Larry as to why I didn't go talk to him.

As Larry queried about one faceless student rushing past or another, I tried not to stare as Tessa came up to Sean, with Brenna on one side and Charlotte on the other. Even though my own gaze was stuck slightly on him, I noticed that Brenna also only looked at him. She tried to catch his eyes and rewarded him with a large, beautiful smile when she succeeded. Tessa looked slightly annoyed at her friend, then slung her arm through his, and the entire group went into the building. Seeing Sean so early in the morning was a bit of a distraction for the day, and I found myself thinking of him more often than I liked.

Larry seemed determined to help with that particular problem as we entered the teeming mass of teenage bodies all trying to swim upstream to whichever class for which they were about to be late. I kept my head down and fought my way through, but Larry didn't need to worry about bumping into someone, so he had plenty of time to look around, and, as silence seemed like it might actually be deadly for him, he kept up a constant stream of commentary.

"Is she a friend? How 'bout him? Gah, not that lad, I hope! He's busy acting the maggot."

That last one caught my attention, so I listened as he gave his opinion on all he saw. He seemed interested in every person at the school, and truth be told, I knew very little about any of them. There were the kids from the French Club, some of whom I had gotten to know somewhat. I could actually tell him a few things about them, but I think he could sense my disinterest and did not bother to disguise his own.

We went through the morning together in a relentless, monotonous rhythm: him asking me about this person and that, me answering him with small shakes of my head or flicking at him in my hair. I couldn't honestly say what, if anything, I learned in my first few classes. I sincerely hoped that nothing of much importance was said. Larry seemed particularly unimpressed with the high school hierarchy. Finally, during Biology, my last class before lunch and one class in which I was not exactly excelling in currently, I just ignored him completely and took notes. He sighed heavily in my ear and said, "Well, this is just biscuits to a bear, slan agat." I grimaced. He was gone, but now I couldn't concentrate on what Mr. Upton was saying as I was too busy figuring out what Larry had said. I assumed one of those two phrases meant goodbye, but I was stumped on the other. The bell rang, and I realized I had missed half a whiteboard of information. *Larry*!

I thought I might have a calmer lunch, but Larry appeared suddenly on my shoulder as I hunched by my locker, putting books away and grabbing my lunch. I sighed and looked up in time to see the French club set walk past me on their way to eat. They nodded at me, and I returned the noncommittal greeting. I sometimes sat with them at lunch, but with Larry hissing in my ear, I felt I would be too distracted, and I'm not sure they were ready to meet insane Mary-Claire. I left the confines of the school building and found a secluded spot outside.

From that vantage point, Larry had a full view of the outdoor student body, and so did I. Sean was there. And so was Tessa; she was almost always by his side. The rest of their entourage was scattered on the prickly grass around them. I wasn't sure if it was my projection onto the group, but Tessa and Sean were always in the center, with even those in the golden group not quite measuring up. I took a bite of my sandwich and forgot to look away.

"Mary-Claire, why don't we go eat with him?" Larry asked, innocence in his voice and mischief in his eyes. I'm pretty sure he had already figured out my relationship with Sean, and that was embarrassing.

"I'm fine eating here. It's in the shade," I said, tucking my legs under me to get them out of the sun they had been enjoying. The food in my mouth turned to paste. I struggled to swallow it as I attempted to focus my gaze on any other group of people anywhere. I failed miserably because I didn't know any other names, and the faces all melded into one giant blob of no one.

"Of course," Larry said solicitously. He was sitting under a shrub, just out of sight of anyone, should anyone look in our direction. But they didn't. We ate in silence for about fifteen minutes, which I found I enjoyed. It's funny how much more enjoyable silence is when there is the possibility of it being broken.

"You know, dear..." Larry began, seemingly not enjoying the silence as much as I did. However, the end-of-lunch bell rang, signaling the beginning of the next period.

"Gotta go," I said, and I grabbed him and placed him in my backpack. I took my time gathering up my lunch trash. I knew I was going to be late for the next class, but I didn't want to rush in next to Sean, Tessa, and their crowd. If I was lying to myself, I would say it was because I was afraid of what Larry might do, but the reality was I just didn't like to be that close to the guy who didn't know I was alive. Too many reminders of what would never be.

Because of that, I was indeed late for algebra; I thought that might be okay because I got in a small amount of trouble, and Larry was respectfully quiet for most of that class. In fact, I thought maybe he just liked hiding in my hair and watching what was going on, and this might be the start of a more bearable afternoon. I was wrong, and after Mr. Mills had begun to explain a tricky formula, I found out how wrong I was. Unfortunately, the silence at lunch had a bad effect on Larry. He now began to keep a near-constant running commentary on anyone and everyone he saw. And because he didn't have to worry about school assignments or even walking, that was every student we passed. So through the rest of my classes, I only half-heard (or quarter-heard, more accurately) what was being taught. I did okay until the last period of the day, English.

"Well, I don't blame you for not getting to know that girl. She's gacky," Larry said in one ear, and my brain tried to figure out who was "gacky" and what "gacky" meant, while Mrs. Montoya said, "Mary-Claire, do you know what Blake was referring to by the 'tyger.'"

I blinked, and the bell rang, and I thought I was saved.

"Mary-Claire, could you please stay after?"

I sighed deeply, and Larry chuckled as he slid into my backpack. "Of course, Mrs. Montoya."

She was one of my favorite teachers, and I hated to disappoint her. She asked if everything was okay, and I tried to respond positively. Apparently, she had tried several times to get a response out of me in class and was worried because I had not answered. She seemed genuinely concerned, so the question/answer session took longer than I had expected. By the time I had convinced her that I had just slept poorly the night before, the buses were pulling out of the parking lot. I was walking again.

"I hope you sleep better tonight dear," Mrs. Montoya said as she walked toward a gloriously air-conditioned car.

I smiled, waved, and then looked off across the open field that I had to cross to get home. My face was already burning a little from yesterday's exposure.

"I wish you could beam me home," I said into my backpack, wondering if that was the best wish to start with.

"HA!" Larry responded, not bothering to come out into the sunshine. I heard him muttering about the brutal sun and wishing he'd been more careful on his rainbow. The line of thought intrigued me, so I asked, "Can you control who sees your rainbow?"

Larry murmured something from the confines of my backpack, and I think he thought that was the end of it. But it was his fault I was walking again, and it was his fault that I was sunburned yesterday. I needed a distraction, so I stopped walking, dropped my backpack on the ground, and knelt beside it; all in an effort to make it look like I was looking for something in it, not talking to a miniature man inside.

"Come on, Larry, I'll dump out the contents and make you ride on my shoulder in the sun. I want to know," I said, with a little more irritation than I intended. I pushed my lunchbox aside and saw green eyes glittering up at me.

"I don't want to come out," Larry said like a petulant child.

"You don't have to. Just answer my question. That's all."

He sighed, heaved himself on top of my math book, and from that precarious perch, said, "Yes and no. When I'm riding my rainbow, it takes on a deeper hue so it can more easily be seen. However, I usually take care of when and where I ride it so that no humans can see. I thought yesterday was a hot enough day, and I didn't notice anyone looking, so I took the chance."

I had slung one shoulder strap over my left shoulder so the opening of the bag balanced closer to my left ear and resumed walking. I still saw no one, so I risked a question.

"Could anyone have seen it?"

"Well, yes and no again. Ya see, that's the other thing I thought made me safe. Only one of Irish Ancestry can see a full visible rainbow, but it seems like these days, everyone has a little bit of Irish, so I should have been more careful. However, more Irish blood than any other country must run through their veins for it to shine brightly. So, you see, dearie, I didn't see any people to begin with, and I certainly didn't expect an Irish Colleen to be traipsing across the field either. Bad luck for both of us."

I wasn't sure how I felt about being called "bad luck," and then I realized he insinuated that I was not only bad luck, but so was he. "Why bad luck for me? You really aren't that bad of a companion, and getting my fondest wishes seems like a dream, thank you."

Larry was silent for a moment and then said softly, "Yes, Colleen, it always *seems* like a dream to begin with." And with that cryptic pronouncement, he dug himself into the innards of my backpack. As he dug himself towards the bottom, I heard him say, "It's not your fondest wish, it's a true wish. Big difference…"

Pondering the meaning of his statements, I walked to the football field without noticing. It probably had to do with muscle memory, as this was the route I took whenever I had to walk home. I hadn't been actively trying to avoid the fields, and that was apparently enough for my body. I wasn't really paying attention, my mind was still caught up in Larry's riddle, but then I heard the whistles of the coaches and shouts of the cheerleaders. I glanced up quickly, first at the girls, my eyes resting on Tessa briefly, but, as always, my gaze sought out Sean.

The players were running drills, and I had a hard time finding him. Weird, you would've thought I could see through the helmets. The hot sun took its toll on everything, including immortal high school football players, and they soon took a water break, I saw his head emerge from his helmet. I didn't even realize Larry could possibly hear me as I whispered while watching the golden god Sean take a long drink.

"I wish he was *my* boyfriend."

I was only barely aware of his body leaping onto my shoulder, but I heard the words in my ear very clearly. "That, love, was a true wish. And it shall be granted. Starting, I think, now."

~Chapter 7~

I wondered what he could possibly mean. I hoped he wouldn't cause some commotion that would call attention to me. I conjured up in my mind something along the lines of Aladdin's triumphal entry into Agrabah, myself sitting atop a bellowing wooly mammoth. The image was so ridiculous that I cringed. And just a second later, I realized that would have been far preferable.

I was just about to ask him what he meant when I realized he wasn't with me anymore. I foolishly felt all around my neck as though I couldn't feel him when he perched on my shoulder. I dropped my backpack to the ground and dug through it. I suddenly felt exposed on the grass and just wanted to go home. But I didn't know if he could find me, and I didn't relish the idea of Larry on the loose for the evening. Reluctantly, I gave up my search and turned back to the field.

As the football players were not doing much, my attention was caught by the loud shouts of the cheerleaders. They were revving up for their showstopper, a six-person pyramid with Tessa on top. Although I was jealous of their popularity, I had to admire the speed and skill with which they formed the pyramid. Three male cheerleaders took their stance on the bottom, Charlotte and another girl clambered quickly on their shoulders, and, finally, Tessa took her triumphant place on top. I felt the very real physical feeling of jealous nausea. I would never command the attention which came so easily to her.

I almost turned away, but then I saw the leg of one of the second-tier girls buckle. It took a half second, and the perfect human shape wobbled slightly. Perched at the top, Tessa, her face turned from arms-flung-up joy to confusion and then, a split second later, to abject terror. And then, from a distance, I watched in horror as Tessa fell from the top of the pyramid. The two girls grabbed out for her, as though in their precarious positions they might be able to break her fall. They held fingertips of fabric for only a second; then, there was a sickening thud as Tessa's body hit the pavement. I couldn't see exactly what happened, but the last nauseating memory I had was her head in the downward position.

There was absolute silence for a second, long enough to not hear Tessa crying out or even moaning. Just silence, and then sheer pandemonium. I sank to the grass, unable to stand any longer. And as I sat, I saw a tiny form racing nimbly towards me. Larry, at last, and he was coming from the direction of the melee.

"You didn't..." I said weakly as he approached, but I knew he had.

"I don't think she'll be girlfriend material anymore," he said, and I felt the bile rise in my throat.

"I didn't..."

"You did, lassie, you just weren't specific. You wished he were your boyfriend. I can't change his feelings with magic, so I'm doing what I can to make that happen."

"I didn't..."

"You need to think ahead, Colleen. I will fulfill all your wishes, but only in the way I see fit."

"I didn't..."

We faced each other in a standoff, then I said quietly, "How?"

Larry smiled as though he were very clever, not the pure embodiment of evil, and said simply, " A little tickle behind the knee…" He looked very pleased with himself. "I didn't think you'd wish so soon. I might be back on me rainbow in no time. Of course, we've only just begun. We'll have to spruce you up now, you're hardly pretty enough to be the girlfriend of a footballer."

I looked into his glittering, demented green eyes. In my horror-fogged eyes, he became the epitome of every childhood monster. A grotesque smile was crinkling his ruddy cheeks and showing very pointed teeth. "I wish her better," I said, barely whispering. If someone, anyone heard me, what would they think? But I didn't care. I didn't care how many other things I wanted in life. I just wanted her to be well, back on top of the pyramid and holding court in the cafeteria again.

"Come now, Mary-Claire. I've already told you that I cannot fix the human body nor change it in any meaningful way. What happens to Tessa-lass next is up to the skilled doctors at whatever hospital they take her."

"She's alive then?" I asked, hopeful.

"I assume, although I would hardly know meself. I'm no doctor, Colleen." He was still smiling, still overjoyed at what he'd accomplished. "Now, seriously, we have to fix you up..."

I picked him up and shoved him roughly into the depths of my backpack. I heard him groan as I smashed him against something, but I couldn't look at his face anymore. The thought of him was more than I could bear. Instead, I looked towards the somber knot of people on the field. Although guilt had begun to gnaw its way through my body, there was one thing of which I was certain, one thing that I could and would cling to in the upcoming months. I never wished this on Tessa.

What's more, I realized, as I stood stone still and completely unnoticed, that she had never done anything to me, nothing good maybe, but nothing bad either. In fact, our interaction had been pretty limited for the entire time we had gone to school together. She had her own likes, dislikes, and interests, and so did I. My self-pity at not being included in the golden crowd had made her seem evil. But now, as I watched classmates, some whose names I knew, some I didn't, rushing around and crying, I was sure that I was the evil one.

Then I saw Sean running from the opposite side of the track straight towards the knot of people. His face was twisted in fear and grief. A few people tried to hold him back, but he pushed through the throng and was quickly absorbed into the mourning mass. Tears coursed down my cheeks. I had *not* wanted this. I hadn't even thought about it on my worst days. I wasn't that kind of monster. But I was, unfortunately, metaphysically chained to a miniature one.

"I don't wish for him anymore," I said, my voice a trembling whisper. There was nobody around me, and even if there had been, they certainly wouldn't have cared, but I was still afraid of someone overhearing. Since I knew what had happened, I was terrorized by the fear of someone else figuring it out, as though it would be possible for anyone to think I had engineered this with the help of a demented leprechaun.

There was a rustle of fabric in my pocket, and Larry stuck his head out. "How noble of you, Mary-Claire, but that's simply not true, and you know it. And you will want him more when this scene is not before your eyes. It's time to go home. I can accept that no more will be accomplished today."

I looked once more toward the sickening scene and heard the distant wail of the ambulance. Without a conscious prompt, my legs began moving slowly across the field. And as I got further away from the stadium, I realized I wanted nothing more than to leave. But as much as I wanted to leave the school grounds, I also wished I knew what was happening with Tessa. Any remnant of bad feeling I had possessed for her was gone. I just wanted her to be fine, to come back to school tomorrow, walk arm in arm with Sean, hobbled slightly by the ace bandage around her ankle. But again, I saw her swan diving to the pavement and knew the bandage would definitely not be around her ankle, even if she were to come back to school tomorrow.

I walked the two miles home silently. I heard Larry muttering and rustling around in my backpack, but I shook it violently a few times, and he stopped. I didn't know what to do now. I wanted out of the deal with the miniature devil, but I wasn't sure there was a loophole. The worst part was I had no one to talk to. I had a few friends/acquaintances at school, but some of them didn't even know my parents were divorced, I could hardly tell anybody the truth of my life right now. On the best of days, my mother was not the coddling type, and her life recently was anything but the best of days. And anyway, even if she had been the bear-huggin' momma of cartoons, I still wouldn't be able to tell her the whole truth.

No, I was alone in this horror movie of a life. No, not entirely alone. I had a tiny man wiggling in my backpack, a dangerous, demonic soul who cared nothing about hurting someone. Nothing about killing either, apparently. So there was that. I felt tears crowding into the corners of my eyes, but I refused myself that comfort. I didn't deserve to cry, and there would be plenty of people crying today who didn't deserve it either.

I got home and found the door unlocked again. I wasn't running that late, and even if she were coming home early, Mom would not be here already. Mike was actually at the table doing his homework, this being the one day ever that I wished he was bent over a computer game oblivious to the world. He looked up over his book and smiled. Seriously, would the parts in my life ever work in symphonic harmony?

"Hi, Mary-Claire! Did you have a good day? Can I have my quesadilla?"

Well, that made more sense at least; it wasn't so much me as the thought of the promised snack. I wanted so badly to tell him no, to throw some snack from the cupboard at him, but that didn't seem fair. I knew my current mood wasn't his fault. Nothing that happened today was his fault. It was all mine, and that was a burden I'd have to carry alone. I mustered up a smile for him.

"Of course, Mikey," I said as I went to the fridge to get the ingredients. "But after, I need to go study, OK?"

I didn't actually expect him to protest, but I needed to be alone as soon as possible. He shrugged, smiled again, and bent back over his homework. It was such a different scene than yesterday that if I hadn't known that Larry lurked in the confines of my backpack, I would have sworn he had something to do with it. I shredded the cheese and cooked up the quesadilla for him.

As I placed the plate in front of him, I hoped his homework would be easy for him this afternoon. I had completed my promised task, and I was not in the mood to help him further. My good intentions would only carry me so far today. I didn't need to worry. As soon as the cheesy goodness was placed before him, he abandoned his homework and started playing video games. On a different day, any different day, I would have put a stop to this immediately, but I took full advantage of the fact that he would be occupied and vaulted up the stairs.

After reaching the blessed solitude of my room, I grabbed a book out of my backpack and tossed it roughly on the bed. I heard a soft grunt from inside but nothing else. Not even muttered cursing. I violently opened the textbook, tearing one of the pages, but I was too distracted to even know what subject it was. I stared blindly at the letters on the page and waited for some inane comment from my fiendish companion, but none was forthcoming. I glanced at the bed and saw him perched silently on the edge. Larry, for his part, seemed to really understand that he just might have, just maybe have, crossed some line today. He watched me study for a little while and then just left. No weird words, no jokes at my expense; he just left. And he didn't return.

While I kept up the charade of studying, I also kept looking for him the entire evening, though not in any sense of anticipation. I dreaded having to look at his face, but I didn't want to be surprised by it either. I was still in a foul mood when I heard the car pulling into the carport. My mom was home, and I had nothing ready for dinner. I didn't want to go face her; I wasn't sure I had any fight left in me, and I was way too close to tears for a confrontation. I went trepidatiously downstairs and was greeted with a pleasant shock. My mom had come home with a pizza; this was a most welcome break from the rest of today. She seemed to be in rough shape too, and we ate at the bar in mostly silence. I guessed the couple didn't buy anything today, but honestly, I didn't much care. Mike threw out some thoughts on his day, but he got no bites, so he eventually fell silent.

At the end of dinner, my mom scooped up the plates and then stopped in front of me.

"Bad day," she said, and it was more a statement of fact than a question.

I looked up at her and nodded. "You too?"

She nodded back. "Do you want to talk about it?"

I shook my head more vehemently than I intended and then raised an eyebrow at her.

She shook her head less violently but still insistent. Great, we were both in agreement. I nodded goodbye to her and parted ways. Yep, no coddling.

Larry didn't show up again until right before I was falling asleep. He came in quietly but cleared his throat to announce his presence. I rolled over in my bed to face away from him.

"Mary-Claire, I…" he paused, and I heard him shuffling nervously, his hands wringing a green and black striped nightcap with a gold buckle emblazoned on it. "I'm sorry. I don't know if I'm sorry for what I did yet, but I'm sorry for how I acted afterward."

I rolled back over to face him. As furious and disgusted as I was, I could tell this apology was sincere and not easy.

"I don't think of humans in the same light as, well, as I guess I do my own kind. I don't think of them as having feelings or …" his voice trailed off again. This was really difficult for him, and I started to feel slightly sorry for him.

"Larry," I began, but he stopped me.

"Please, Mary-Claire, let me finish. The only humans I tend to care about are the ones to whom I get stuck, and only a precious few of them. The rest are just annoying giants. But I realize that today I shouldn't have laughed. I shouldn't have been happy about what happened. I still feel it necessary, but I should have had more respect. She's alive, Mary-Claire."

At this pronouncement, I sat up in bed. "She is? Are you sure? How do you know?"

He smiled slightly at me, "I've been checking. I have my ways. I...I thought you might like to know at least that news. She's alive. She is not well; I won't lie about that, but she is alive."

I wanted to still be angry, and I was slightly I guess, but I felt that the leprechaun apology was probably a rare thing. I knew he meant every word.

"Thank you, Larry," I said simply and sincerely before rolling back over to go to sleep.

~Chapter 8~

Morning came, and while I was less angry than I thought I would be, I still found myself dreading the idea of school. I knew what happened to Tessa would be the talk of the place, and I didn't think I could handle it. And since there was no one who could possibly understand why I was so affected by it, I felt inadequate for that particular torture. I decided not to go to school, but that decision didn't make my morning any better.

It turned out that waking up in a semi-not-bad mood was going to be short-lived for me, and it wasn't just because of tortured, half-remembered dreams of Tessa. After the haze of sleep evaporated, I recognized that it wasn't the electronic beep of an alarm that broke through my fitful sleep. It was worse. I woke up to the sound of my mother crying, which also meant that I had woken up a half hour or so before my alarm was set to go off. I knew this because for the past six months, like clockwork, if I woke up too early, I could hear my mother crying through the thin walls of the apartment. I hated my father every morning when this happened, and it was always a lousy way to start the day. My tepid humor was beginning to go sour.

This development was helped along by Larry. I rolled over to check the time, and I saw his face beaming, his emerald eyes gleaming. His sincere apology given last night, I think he'd assumed we'd be ready for business today. We wouldn't be, well, *I* wouldn't be. And oddly, I wasn't as happy as I thought I'd be to disappoint him. So I tried my best to ignore him. It wasn't easy.

"Oh, Mary-Claire, what a day today will be! You must look your best," he said as he hopped all over my bed, trying to catch my eye as I studiously tried to avoid his. He was more nimble than I and so eventually positioned himself right where he needed to be. He didn't say anything, but his grin said everything; his grin and his green beret with a black tassel and gold buckle rakishly off to the side.

I sighed heavily, probably just a bit overly dramatically, to let him know how much I truly disliked the whole idea, "What are you talking about?"

If he picked up on anything I was laying down, he certainly didn't act like it. "Well, dear, a fine thing like Sean will only stay single for so long. You must make your move right now. Get up, get up!"

I rolled so my back was to him and, for extra emphasis, put a pillow over my head, ignoring his words and then his tiny hands pummeling my back. Did he honestly think I would do that? Even with his repentant act yesterday, did he think I was going to get dressed up and sashay through the halls looking for Tessa's boyfriend? The very day after her accident, did he honestly think I was going to run to school, march up to Sean, and declare my love for him? Stupid leprechaun in a stupid beret! Like I would take relationship or fashion advice from the gaudiest mime ever!

"Mary-Claire, get up!" his Irish lilt came from somewhere near my right shoulder blade. I rolled over quickly and was vaguely amused to see how fast he had to scamper out of the way before getting crushed.

"C'mon ya gowl, there's no time to waste. I said I was sorry for what happened, but you wished for it, not me," he said, huffing a little as he tried desperately to pry my body from my mattress. To be honest, I was a little surprised he wasn't able to do it. I thought maybe super strength was going to end up being one of the traits of the little people. How the heck was I supposed to know the rules for supernatural creatures?

"I did NOT want this to happen! I never wanted anything to happen to Tessa."

I actually shouted the last few words and realized my mistake because my mother stopped crying in her room immediately. I glared at Larry, and he glared back. We were still locked grumpily in this stalemate when five minutes later, time enough to compose herself, she knocked on my door.

"Mary-Claire, honey, are you ok in there?"

"I'm fine Mom," I said as Larry and I broke our impasse, and he scurried behind my clock.

He was hidden none too soon either because he had just barely made it to safety when she pushed the door open. "Mary-Claire, I heard you shouting. Who's Tessa?"

I took a deep breath. Lying was never my strong suit, but I was realizing more and more that I was going to have to get more adept at it since Larry came to town. And in this instance in particular, it was vitally important. However, I could see the advantage of this current situation and hoped my brain could keep up with what I needed from it. I faced my mom and took in the red-rimmed blue eyes and blotchy skin from her morning mourning, and I felt even worse about lying. So I looked away and hoped that this act, in and of itself, wouldn't give me away for the prevaricator that I was.

"She's a girl in my school, and she had a terrible accident yesterday," I said slowly, the story building in my mind. "I saw it happen." I paused to let my mom gasp and sit on the bed. "It was really awful. I don't want to go to school today. I'll go tomorrow, but I had nightmares all night about it, and I just don't feel up to school today." I still couldn't look at her, but I could lean in and let myself take in her flowery scent.

"Of course, sweetie, if that's what you need," she said, stroking my hair. Boy, I must have sounded really upset when I yelled at Larry. She was pulling out all the old, not-too-busy-for-you mom cards. I almost expected her to offer to stay home with me, an offer I would have accepted with alacrity. But the next thing she said was, "Will you be alright alone all day? I have so many showings today. I really think I might sell a house."

I turned to face her and tried desperately not to let my disappointment show on my face. I hadn't realized how much I had wanted her to stay until she said that. But the flash of ruddy whiskers by my clock made me realize that today would be just Larry and me, and I was not looking forward to that combination.

"Yes, I'll be fine. Just don't forget to call me in." I lowered my head after that. I was afraid her eyes could see through me, and I was especially afraid she would see the lies written all over my face. Plus, she looked so deeply sad. I think my need for her added to her melancholy and I hated myself for that, despite the fact that I couldn't stop wishing for it.

My mom kissed the top of my head, and my heart lurched for a second. I missed that mom. "I won't honey, I promise. Hey, I'm sorry I can't take the whole day off, but do you want breakfast?" I heard the almost wistful tone of her voice, and I was surprised that she sounded like she would actually prefer to stay home with me.

I actually didn't want breakfast, I wasn't sure if I could keep anything down, but I had been making my own breakfasts for six months, mine and Mike's, so if she was offering, I would eat. Besides, my mom made the best pancakes, and it had been a while since I'd had them.

I looked up as she left the room, and she flashed one more sympathetic smile in my direction. I smiled back as best I could and then turned to face one angry leprechaun.

"I really think, my dear, 'tis a mistake for you to miss today," Larry said, his voice tight but not furious.

"I really think that you need to lay off for a day," I said, looking at him in his tiny green eyes. Neither of us blinked. I was getting much better at our staring contests.

Finally, he sighed heavily, blinked exaggeratedly, and said, "If I'm letting you go today, just know that tomorrow I'll expect results."

I gave him a half smile and turned away. He could expect anything that made him happy, I wasn't going to produce today, tomorrow, or next year. I could not allow myself to capitalize on Tessa's accident. I didn't want to be that person, but that was definitely an argument for another time, hopefully another day.

I was not a good person that morning. Even knowing how hard it was for her to rearrange her morning and that, once she got to work, she had a full day ahead of her, I took full advantage of my mother's compassion. This, of course, only served to compound my guilt. I knew that I had caught her in a particularly weakened state, in the midst of her tears, and part of her niceness had root directly in her own depression and inability to take the day off. But the horror of yesterday hardened my mind and heart, and I just pushed out any feeling that made its way in.

My mom brought me breakfast in bed, her special pancakes, breakfast sausage, and two glasses, one of orange juice and one of milk, just like every good commercial breakfast ever. I made a good show of eating them until I heard the car engine. Then my stomach revolted and I put the plate on my bedside table. At least Mike would have also gotten a good breakfast.

Hearing the car, Larry jumped right up and broke off a piece of pancake. It looked laughably large in his tiny fist, but the sight of it just made me angry. "Well Mary-Claire, your mam is quite a cook! Too bad she doesn't have more time."

"Yeah, too bad," I said over my shoulder as I headed into the bathroom. The one place I knew he wouldn't follow me. I took a long hot shower, which aggravated my sunburn, but I felt I deserved that pain. I stayed in so long that the water became colder and colder, until I was shivering. I got out and methodically dried off. I wanted as much alone time as possible. When I was completely dry, I dressed and fussed with my hair for another fifteen minutes. I didn't bother with makeup as I didn't plan on going anywhere. Finally, I stayed in the tiny room as long as I could stand. I opened the door, and Larry was standing right outside.

"Honestly, Mary-Claire. I'm sorry," he said, and his face once again looked sincere. Maybe leprechaun apologies weren't as rare as I had thought. This was far from comforting, as it meant there were going to be plenty of things for which he was going to need to apologize.

"About Tessa this time?" I said, towering over him and irritated. If he wasn't going to be sorry about her, then there was no need to keep apologizing.

"Well, I suppose," he said, his forehead wrinkled in confusion as though the thought of wasting emotion on a random human being was more than he could understand. Then his forehead relaxed, and he looked at me and said sincerely, "I'm mostly sorry I've upset you so badly. I'm just trying to make your wish come true. You really have to remember when you wish that I don't give much thought to any other human than the one I'm indentured to. I cannot promise I won't do something similar again, but understand, my only loyalty is to you and giving you your wishes. Once I've completed our bargain, I'm free and so are you."

It wasn't exactly the gushing apology I'd been hoping for, but it did make sense, and it seemed as sincere as the one last night. Besides, I found both of these apologies better than if he had prostrated himself at my feet and begged for forgiveness. That seemed totally out of character for my companion and would have been more for show than for real sorrow. I was beginning to realize that I was going to have to accept the current circumstances and go forward.

"I guess I understand, but I would *never* have wished her harm," I said, hoping to get through to him that harming another human was untenable.

"Ah, yes, but your wish could only be carried out if she were out of the way, and I saw an opportunity. I knew it wouldn't kill her, or at least I was pretty sure. Honestly you humans are quite fragile for how large you are. I sometimes forget that."

I hated how matter-of-fact he sounded. I had been thinking of him as a tiny person, a tiny *human,* but I realized in that second that he was not human; he was something else altogether. It seemed odd, but then I understood that it was the most normal explanation of what had happened. He was not human, he did not have human feelings, human emotions, or human inhibitions. I was going to have to be very careful what I wished for from here on out, *if* I wished for anything at all. I might just have a leprechaun companion for life.

Larry and I had a semi-nice day together. We had come to a shaky truce that, just for today, we would not talk about Sean, Tessa, or anything to do with my wish. Larry seemed to get that whatever imaginary line in my head he had crossed had been too far. So, once we were positive we were alone, we camped out on the couch and watched terrible daytime TV. Since all things human seemed to both befuddle and amuse him, the worse the talk show, the more he enjoyed it. And it turns out a highly amused leprechaun is an extraordinarily funny companion.

"I vote he is the da!" he shouted directly to the TV. He stared intently as the two guests, or "contestants" to Larry, argued their case. He didn't move until the commercials started. "Is that how this works? Who gets the final vote, and what do they win if the stick turns blue?"

I laughed at his mixing the show with the inevitable commercials that run with such travesty. "Science gets the final vote, and that guy wins a lifetime of being hooked to her," I said, thinking of the loud-mouthed, big-haired woman who had been screaming loudly that he was the only possibility for father. Absolutely. Probably.

"That's a *win*? Why take the test?"

"Why find the end of the rainbow? Because nobody knows what's really going to happen," I said, but I smiled widely at him so that he would know, for at least the time being. I was kidding.

Larry smiled back at me. "Well, the end of the rainbow is a better bet. Only a few leprechauns I know can shout like that scab. And three wishes later, you'll say goodbye to me!"

I frowned slightly at the mention of wishes, but I had started this jesting, and he had only taken it to its natural end. So, I shook my head to clear the irritation and said with imperial inflection, "I wish for lunch."

"Hah!" was his only reply. And then a huge belly laugh when the host grandly proclaimed the guy was not the father. He laughed even harder when the lucky not-baby-daddy started doing a touchdown dance as the woman zoomed around the studio, screaming that the test couldn't be correct. "I still canna tell whether he won or not!"

We spent a few more hours delving into the underbelly of humanity, but then I decided I should attempt to accomplish something. I cracked a book or two, but there was nothing pressing at school, and I didn't have the inclination for it today. Although Larry was still being entertained by the TV, there's only so much of it I can take. I sighed, looked around the house, and finally found a project in cleaning out the pantry. This task had the dual benefit of taking a large amount of time and providing me with a list of ingredients for dinner.

By the time Mike came home I had finished cleaning and commenced baking. He was first shocked to see me and then outraged that I had been granted permission to skip school for no discernible reason. I had anticipated this reaction, so while Larry scurried up the stairs, he had been far too engrossed in the televised drama to leave before Mike came barreling in, I proffered a plate of placating chocolate chip cookies. Mike was nothing if not predictable. He took three cookies and tried to find some gadget to entertain himself, but I insisted he do his homework, especially if he wanted to keep all three cookies. The age-old war of food versus entertainment played out in his preteen brain, with the good basic food winning. He kept the cookies, grabbed another one when he thought I wasn't watching, and sat down to work on his math.

I kept him company while I cooked dinner. To be truthful, I acted as a tutor while cooking, but I didn't mind. It was actually a pleasant way to spend the early evening. He and I were just finishing up when my mom walked in. I'm not sure what she expected to find, but I think this scene of domestic bliss was last on the list. She looked haggard, and I decided against asking about her day, instead plated her food as she slumped into a chair. We all sat down to a quiet, but not painfully so, meal. Actually, given the rude awakening I had experienced this morning, it was a better day than anticipated, but what would tomorrow bring?

~Chapter 9~

The peace of the day before permeated my dreams, so I woke up the next morning and only kind of wanted to stay in bed. The day immediately started better than the previous one because I woke up to the incessant beep of my alarm and so was not reminded of my mother's misery. As I sat up and blinked at the sharp sunlight, I caught sight of Larry curled into an impossibly small ball on one of the lime green throw pillows from my bed. He looked cute, the way all things small are cute. It was disarming, but also reminded me that he wasn't awful all of the time. So, I decided I just had to face life with my own personal demon and find a way to deal with it. I showered and got dressed in time to make it down for a quick toaster waffle breakfast with my mother and brother.

They both treated me with kid gloves for the first half of the meal, but my somewhat buoyant mood must have convinced them that I was okay, and we talked about our upcoming day. My brother was still in his relationship with that girl at school. And he was still just as confused about it. I think the lucky girl who marries him will just have to put a tux on him and tell him that he proposed, and she'll be stuck with that prize. My mom looked rested, and she seemed ok. Not exactly excited for today, but better than yesterday. She was dressed in lilac, from blouse to shoe, and the light color gave her a pseudo air of joy. As she had since the divorce, she had her moment of despair, and now she would come out swinging!

Larry didn't make an appearance for most of the morning. He didn't come around much when I was with my family; I have to admit I was grateful for that small favor. I think they might have noticed if I was constantly talking to myself and, especially, how often I suddenly started arguing with myself. I did worry about his eating, though, so I surreptitiously took a quarter piece of waffle, complete with sticky syrup dripping down my hand, upstairs. It was too bad I knew my mom would notice a plate going upstairs.

When I opened my door, Larry was sitting on my windowsill, staring out at the metallic turquoise sky. He was so still that he seemed more of a figurine than a living thing. I hesitated, not knowing if I was interrupting something.

"Goodness Mary-Claire, how do you live in such bright sunshine?" he said, not turning to look at me. His gaze was fixed on the expansive blue. I glanced out the window and thought I saw the wisp of a rainbow. It was so light and disappeared so quickly that I wasn't sure, although Larry stayed focused on the sky.

"Sunscreen and air conditioning," I said. "Would you like something to eat?"

That got his attention. He smiled when he saw the sticky treat, although even a quarter piece now looked way too big. "My, that looks gorgeous!" he said and, with one more longing glance at the sky, hopped down from the window.

I placed the waffle on a piece of lined paper on my desk. It wasn't the most hygienic place to eat, but as I watched him dive into it, I realized it wasn't going to last long enough to matter. In fact, he had the entire thing eaten before I had packed my backpack. That process was hindered slightly by the syrup I had to lick off my fingers. I suppose that I could have washed my hands, but my mom's homemade syrup was the only vestige from yesterday, and I wasn't going to waste it.

"To be sure, lass, there are some wonderful things you humans have created! Almost all of them are edible, but some very wonderful things, nonetheless. Thank you very much for your kindness. You are a very different person than you presented yourself at our first meeting."

"Yes, well, meeting a supernatural being can do that to a person," I said, and then, "Hang on, what did you think of me when we met?"

Larry smiled and licked the sticky goodness off his own fingers. "Ya seemed pretty selfish. Your questions are so focused on you. But I got ya wrong Colleen, totally wrong. I see that now. You're very caring for your ma and that daft brother of yours. Plus, I don't think you knew the lass Tessa as well as you put on, but you truly did care about her, about what happened to her."

I looked at him, puzzled. "Isn't that the normal reaction? I mean, how well do you have to know someone before you're expected to care?"

He looked back somberly at me, "Oh Mary-Claire, I've granted the wishes of so many humans through the years. Tis sad to say that not as many as you might think care about others. That's one reason I meself may not have been as nice as I could have been. You might have noticed I wasn't so charming at first."

"I noticed," I said. "You were kind of scary sometimes. I thought I was doing something wrong, which, I guess, is fair."

He shook his head thoughtfully. "It really wasn't you, Colleen. It was my previous master," he spat the last word out like it was rotten food. Then his eyes grew sad, and he stared off into the distance, "Oh, the last one I served was a right Jackeen! I wasn't relishing another go with one like that."

He looked truly disgusted. I frowned, wondering what the one before me had wished for while simultaneously trying to figure out if that was an actual insult, but I saw the clock and realized that, once again, I was running behind. I picked up my backpack and held it open in front of him.

"Come on, get in and stay quiet, I think they're both still home, and if I miss the bus again today, my mom's going to have a fit. Oh, hey, *Jackeen*?" I asked as he scurried in.

Larry smiled, "What you Americans might call a real jerk." As he disappeared into the confines, I heard him say in his best American accent, "Yo dude, that homie was a real jerk for..." and I lost the rest. I couldn't help smiling as I carefully slung the pack over one shoulder.

The bus ride felt quieter than normal. Although the regular amount of noise was coming from the teenagers all around me, I found I half missed the constant hiss of Irish idioms in my ear. And, per usual, I sat alone. Enough kids had cars at my school, so the bus was only three-quarters full at best. This meant that nobody had to sit next to the weird new girl, in spite of the fact that I wasn't so very new, and truth be told, I didn't feel so very weird. I suppose the real problem was that, at sixteen, I could be driving—as if we had money for any luxuries, much less a car for the teenage daughter—and so there were hardly any kids my age. At least, this was one of the many things I told myself to keep from becoming totally depressed. It was true, though. I honestly didn't recognize a single kid on my bus from any of my classes. I had thought that Larry might take advantage of the space around me, but he stayed hidden in my backpack, which, as was becoming customary, was simultaneously both a blessing and a curse.

When the bus finally pulled into the large circular bus parking, the school felt a bit surreal. Although things had appeared normal on the ride, once everyone congregated together, the whole student body started crying as one. I found this odd because, honestly, how many of them truly knew Tessa anyway? I knew why I kept feeling like bursting into tears, but as I watched several of the French geeks, I had kind of gotten to know since joining French Club pass with red-rimmed eyes and snotty noses, I wondered if any of them had actually talked to Tessa in the last few days, weeks or months. As far as I could remember, they had never even mentioned her name. Now they couldn't seem to imagine the school without her.

"Wow, Mary-Claire, seems like you wished harm on the most popular girl in school," Larry said, his pleasant Irish lilt scraping on my nerves like skin on asphalt. Oh sure, now that I was surrounded by people, now is when he picked to come out. Honestly, would he never learn to read the room?

"Shut up," I said, keeping my head down and my voice low. I couldn't have anyone seeing me talking to myself. I was hardly popular enough to get past "girl who talks to herself." And yet, with all my non-cherished anonymity since I moved here, I was sure today would be the day someone would notice me. "You know I didn't do this. You did."

"Now, now, that's not nice," Larry said, his voice sounding more amused than hurt. All the conciliatory gestures from yesterday seemed forgotten. How I hated him right now, and he didn't notice at all. "Oh look, Mary-Claire, there's Sean-o. Let's go say hi."

I looked up and saw Sean surrounded by his teammates and cheerleaders, his eyes were red, but he looked more under control than most of the school. Next to him, Brenna leaned on his arm. She had tears streaming down her cheeks, but her face didn't look sad, not really. There might have been some real sorrow there, but if anything, she looked pleased with herself as she clung to him. Her mouth was turned down appropriately, but her brown eyes sparkled as she looked at him. Off to the side, Charlotte slumped against the lockers. She didn't raise her head, and I could see her shoulders shaking quietly. That made me wonder why Sean wasn't crying, but then I caught his eye for a second, and I saw sadness in them, to such a degree that I knew he didn't need to make a big show for people to know how he felt. I looked quickly away.

"Go talk to him," Larry hissed in my ear. "There's obviously some girls who aren't waiting for the wake." I reached up, ostensibly to tuck a strand of red curl behind my ear, but when I got near my neck, I flicked Larry on the head.

"I'm not going to talk to him. Your horrible little trick won't work, you troll," I said.

Larry hissed in my ear, "Hey! There's no need for name-calling, Mary-Claire. I may not be the best-looking 'chaun, but I'm sure no troll! And you'd best be thankful for that because I will be with you until I fulfill three true wishes, and you wouldn't want to get stuck with an ugly, smelly troll for a friend forever. Now go and talk to Sean."

I ducked my head, hoping this would keep people from seeing my mouth moving, and whispered furiously, "I told you I'm not going near him."

I heard Larry sigh heavily. "Colleen, I dinna mean to sound so cheesed off, but I can't get back to me rainbow until I fulfill your three wishes. And I so miss her." With that, he leaped off my shoulder and disappeared somewhere in the crowd. I watched for a brief moment, but for a little guy, he was really fast.

After he vanished, I realized that I didn't know where he was going, nor did I particularly care. Having no friends to talk to was supremely better than having him whispering in my ear at all times. That thought comforted me for a few seconds until I accidentally made eye contact with another of the cheerleaders. She looked grief-stricken, and I was sure she saw a mirrored look in my own because she gave me a wan smile before slipping into the throng of teenagers rushing to class. After that, I kept my head down, not wanting to make eye contact with anyone else, just in case I might see what harm I had done to another person.

The day passed slowly, agonizingly slow. In nearly every class, the teacher started the day by announcing that there would be grief counselors available all week should anyone need to talk. In truth, by about third period, I was getting a little sick of the whole thing. I mean, yes, what happened was terrible, truly deeply tragic, but she wasn't dead for crying out loud. She was still unconscious, but she wasn't dead. And, of greater import, she had not been everybody's friend. I think I would have dealt with everything better if it weren't for all the people who suddenly needed counseling. More and more, I noticed, as teachers gave anyone a pass to leave class for counseling but failed to walk them there. By my fourth hour, I had seen at least six people who had left class for "counseling" walking in the grassy courtyard. Teachers were clueless, and teenagers would always be the worst. Motto for the day.

This was confirmed for me as I walked to lunch. As I trudged along through the mass of humanity, I heard some kids snickering to the side of me. I glanced over quickly and saw at least one kid from my science class who had "needed" counseling. Ugh.

"How many cheerleaders does it take to make a pyramid? Six, and five to make a vegetable." Gales of laughter.

I felt nauseous. Sometimes I was glad not to have friends here. I was surprised how many times today I had gone back and forth on the same issue. Larry was not having a good effect on my mental stability. But for now, I was coming down firmly on the side of no friends would be better than these idiots.

Oddly, even with the "tragedy" that no one could seem to go a minute without needing counseling for, the lunchroom was its usual hive of activity. I got my food and found some of the same girls from the French club, who had been so swollen-eyed this morning, sitting and laughing at a table. I wouldn't say we were exactly friends, but I sat next to them at some lunches. It did make things more bearable, and I was relatively certain they wouldn't make the same sick jokes. They may not have been my closest confidants, but they weren't awful people. I didn't think I could take any more of those horrible "jokes," and I couldn't stand being alone with my thoughts anymore.

"Mary-Claire, did you hear about Tessa?" a blonde girl named Emma asked.

I bit back a sharp retort about not living under a rock and answered stiffly but politely, "Yes, they've talked about it in most of my classes."

Emma's hazel eyes got wide and excited as she prepared to launch into gossip, "I heard it happened a couple of days ago, right after school."

Minni, a small, dark-haired girl who usually sat in the corner said, "I heard it was awful, so much blood!"

The girls all did a theatrical "Ooooooh" to this, and I couldn't stop myself from saying, "No, not really. Just a loud thump."

As soon as I said it, I wished I hadn't. First, the word "thump" seemed disrespectful, although I couldn't put my finger on why. Second, because I became an instant celebrity at the table, including the group of four at the end, whose names and faces I couldn't place but who now found me fascinating.

"You were *there?*" Emma said, inhaling sharply.

"Did you see it happen?" a guy from the end of the table asked quickly.

"Umm, yes, I was walking home when it happened."

There was absolute silence as they all waited for the gory, literally, details. I looked out at the rapt audience I had and suddenly felt sick to my stomach. They had all been crying this morning for their "dear friend," and now they wanted a blow-by-blow of what happened, complete with sound effects, if I could possibly produce them.

I felt the tears prick in my eyes as I said quickly, "I'm sorry, but I can't. It was awful enough to see without trying to remember and describe it."

I turned to leave and found myself face-to-face with Sean and some of his friends. They were all looking at me, and I wondered how much they had heard. I ducked my head and made my way out of the lunchroom, but not before seeing...what in Sean's eyes...gratitude at my discretion? Was that it? Well, at least Larry hadn't been around to see it; he would have loved it.

~Chapter 10~

I zombie-walked through the rest of the day, not looking around and just trying to get to the final bell without becoming another quasi-celebrity. Even while keeping my head low, I saw that anybody who knew anything about the accident was surrounded by willing listeners. Revolting. I went to the office with stomach cramps during French. They miraculously healed themselves when the hour was over. Finally, the blessed bell rang, and I had successfully navigated the minefield of sickly sad students.

With school finally over, I started home, deciding to ditch the bus again today. I was getting used to walking home after the past few days. It was remarkably peaceful, and I was actually getting used to the sun. Moreover, I didn't want to ride the bus with all the faux grieving that was sure to be going on inside. And, as a final nail in the bus-coffin, Minni sometimes rode my bus home. I was sure the fact that I had been an eyewitness would be known by everyone before I even set foot in the vehicle. So, I opted for a solo jaunt across the backfield. I wasn't afraid of seeing Sean practicing; both the cheerleaders and the football team had called a recess for the last two days.

As I broke free from the remaining students, all headed to either bus or car, I realized I had not seen Larry since that morning. I wondered idly if I should be concerned. He kept saying that he couldn't leave me, but he also seemed to be making up the rules as he went along. Maybe he could actually leave a particularly stubborn human. Or maybe he got squashed in the sea of feet he would've had to navigate. That thought made me startlingly sad. I had convinced myself this morning that I didn't like him, but I realized now that I did like him, maybe just a little. I started looking around for any sign of him.

As I entered the empty track, a small wind blew and picked some of my papers out of my backpack. I must have forgotten to close it after my last class. Maybe I hadn't closed it the whole day after my fight with Larry. I really couldn't remember most of the day, and what parts I could, I wanted to forget. My concern for Larry gave way to irritation. Although it wasn't rational, I felt better blaming Larry for the unzipped backpack than myself. I had enough to feel guilty about. Stupid Larry, I thought viciously; even when he isn't with me, he causes trouble.

I chased the papers as they blew across the track and over the field, finally coming to rest under the opposing metal bleachers. I looked back where I had come from and, to my relief, saw no one. How stupid I must have looked running after loose-leaf papers. Then I looked forward and saw Sean sitting with his back against a metal post, head down. I tried not to breathe, but he looked up anyway.

"Do you mind..." he said quietly.

"Oh no, I was just grabbing some of my papers. I'm leaving now."

"No, do you mind sitting and talking for a minute? I just need someone to talk to."

"Then why are you here?" I asked, instantly wishing my brain had a stupid question filter. But I wasn't going to stay anyway; no way I was letting Larry win in this one. I had convinced myself that I was giving up on Sean. So, Larry would have to deal with the fact that he hurt Tessa for no reason. And he would have to find another way to get back to his rainbow.

"Because I'm tired of the pitying looks from everyone. The whole school has been staring at me the same way all day; but now that I'm alone, I just want someone to talk to," he said, looking at me so sadly that I almost decided to stay.

"I'm sorry, but I'm supposed to be home soon. I have to watch my little brother after school," I said, backing away slowly as I word-vomited my life for Sean. Funny how the one thing I'd wanted for a year now held little interest to me.

"Please Mary-Claire, I could really use the company."

The use of my name stopped my escape. Did he know my name? Since when? I don't remember a single conversation with him in Trig last year.

"I'm Sean, by the way, Sean Flannery. I don't know if you remember me or not. We had Trigonometry last year together, for the month or so you were there before summer."

The words weren't exactly in another language, but they also didn't compute in my brain. He was introducing himself as though there might be someone in the school who didn't know who he was.

"I remember," I said. "But your name is in the school paper more than mine, so I'm surprised you know who I am."

Sean smiled slightly. "Mary-Claire is an unusual name."

I smiled back, then looked around quickly for a sliver of emerald green. I would stay, but only if Larry weren't around. He didn't need to know this was happening. Stupid demented leprechaun. I saw nothing out of place in the cement walkway we were on or anywhere nearby. I shoved my papers in my backpack and rummaged roughly through it to make sure Larry wasn't hiding in it. Satisfied the green demon had nothing to do with the current situation, I focused back on Sean.

"So, how are you doing with all this?" I asked, nothing else more enlightening coming forth from my brain.

"You know, it's funny, people have been asking me that for the past two days, like I'm the one who got hurt, like I'm the one in the hospital. I don't get it. I'm fine, nothing happened to me."

"That's not true," I said, setting my backpack down, with one more quick glance inside just to make sure Larry hadn't stealthily climbed in somewhere between the school and here, a girl can't be too careful, and then sitting down close to him, but being careful not to be *too* close. "Obviously, you're not physically hurt, but come on."

He looked at me and nodded his head. "Yeah, I guess, but it feels weird to have people worried about me. Of course, nobody can ask Tessa."

I cringed at the words. No, no one could ask Tessa because I had made a stupid wish in front of a demonic creature. "Is she still in a coma then?"

"Yeah. And it's not looking good. There was a lot of brain swelling, so the doctors think she'll be permanently disabled, but to what degree they don't know. Or won't say."

He didn't look at me but off towards the track where it happened. I avoided looking that way, but I didn't want to stare at the side of his face, so I looked toward the empty field and my home. I wish I hadn't chased those papers now. I could redo the homework, but this was weird and painful and…much too close to the wish I had made.

"Did you know her well?"

I realized he was looking at me again, so I turned back. "Um, no, not really. But she seemed nice enough."

"You know, that's the most honest answer I've gotten today. Everyone else I've asked seems to be trying to create connections from any interaction they've ever had with her. That's the weirdest part of this, everyone at the school seems to be so upset, and yet, I don't think she had that many friends here last week," he said and paused. Then he looked up, his dark blue eyes looking directly into mine, "So, why do you seem so upset then?"

That question was one that hardly seemed answerable. Why was I so upset? Because I had inadvertently wished this into being. Because sitting and talking to Sean Flannery was something I had dreamed of for so long, the words that put Tessa in a coma had slipped out of my mouth before I thought them. But I couldn't tell him any of this. Even if there wasn't some ancient rule about it, how in the world do you tell someone that you have a leprechaun companion who granted a wish in a really horrific way?

"I saw it happen." I heard the words before I realized I was speaking. Sometimes my brain on autopilot is better than other times. "I was walking home across the field, and I-I just saw it. It's kind of hard to forget something like that, and I guess I feel a part of it somehow." I shook my head, "That doesn't make any sense."

"Actually," he said, "that makes more sense than why most people are acting like this affects them."

He smiled at me, and I smiled back, more out of social conditioning than that this situation made me happy at all. He looked at his watch, then suddenly stood up.

"I'm sorry, but I'm supposed to go to the hospital at four. Her dad is waiting there for me, and we're going to see her together. Thanks for talking with me. I really needed it. See you later Mary-Claire."

He was gone with a wave, and I watched him go, feeling traitorous. I wanted to pretend I didn't enjoy it at all, but that was a complete lie. Oh well, it was one time. This little tete-a-tete was not to happen again. I would make sure of it. But meeting him had given me an idea, something to help ease the ponderous weight of the guilt that I carried. I jerked up my backpack and started for home.

~Chapter 11~

Mike was waiting for me when I walked through the door. So was Larry. He was standing perfectly still beside the plants in the window. I supposed if you were a brainless eleven-year-old, you might actually believe that he was a statue. I, of course, recognized him right away. The sly wink he gave me wasn't necessary. I was so surprised to see him out in the open, but more than that, and I was also shocked to see his green Chiquita banana turban–in a dark green and black camo pattern, although the gold buckle would probably give his position away to the space shuttle–filled with succulents. I assumed he was going for concealment, but now he was the only thing I could see. I was so distracted by the sight I didn't hear what Mike was saying at first.

"Maarrryyy-Claaiirree," Mike said my name with such exaggeration that I nearly smiled. But his face looked angry, and I knew I was a little later than normal. I didn't need to risk his wrath today.

"What, bud?" I asked, ignoring the green figurine in the corner.

"Why are you late today?" he asked, and I could see that he was really upset, not just irritated. I'd better do some damage control.

"I ran into…" I forced myself not to look in Larry's direction as I almost spilled the beans about meeting a friend. I knew Larry would pick up on that and pry until he got the full deets, "a teacher after school. I forgot an assignment. What's wrong?" All of it was lame, but Mike didn't seem to notice, and I wasn't looking at Larry, so I didn't know if he bought it or not.

"I have a project due tomorrow, and I forgot about it too. Mom's going to kill me, kill both of us if I don't get it done."

"Seriously, Mike? What the heck?" I didn't feel capable of this tonight, but apparently, that didn't matter to the universe.

"You can't be mad at me. You did it too!" he said, looking me in the eye.

"I nev..." and then I remembered my lie from a minute ago. Freak. I've got to get better at lying. Or at least remembering my lies. "Right, then, I guess we'd better get to work on yours." I looked over at the living statue and saw interest in his eyes. Great, he picked up on all that. I met his eyes and said, "I *truly* wish your project was done."

Larry started laughing silently. He held his belly and shook. I thought even Mike might have noticed that, but he was winging his way upstairs. "I truly wish it was done too, but I don't think that's going to work," he flung behind as he ran for whatever it was he needed.

Larry doubled over at this and outright laughed. "Oh, that one knows better than you how this works, that's for sure."

I looked at him. "Well, I think I truly want it. I mean, I truly don't want to work on it tonight, so shouldn't that count?"

Larry looked at me soberly. "One rule for me, Mary-Claire, and this is one that canna get around, is that I must fulfill one wish before the next. So even though I do believe that ya truly want a finished plant cell, you'll be on your own for this one, I think."

I frowned. That was a wrinkle I wasn't expecting. I guess I was hoping I could just keep wishing until I got to three finished tasks. Then he wouldn't have to do the first one. I also wondered how he was going to complete the current one. Was he going to have to do more? Was my wish going to have a body count?

Larry saw my frown and shrugged his tiny shoulders. "I don't have many rules that bind me, but this is one that I canna do anything about. The other is that I will be by your side until three true wishes are fully done."

"So not quite a bottle, but..." I said, smiling, trying to bring some levity to the conversation. Larry started briefly and then answered with a wan smile of his own. "True, but I can at least take my leave of you every now and then."

That brought the entire day to mind. "Yeah, hey, where'd you go anyways?"

Larry smiled bigger, "Did ya miss me lass? I thought maybe you had had enough of me for one day. You were very unhappy with me this morning."

I nodded thoughtfully. "I was. But I guess I did miss you a little."

"You did? I missed you too. Sometimes I wish we were in the same school so I could see you."

I whirled around and saw Mike with a small Styrofoam ball, markers, construction paper, toothpicks, and glue. Good heavens, did he have a craft store upstairs? Then I looked into his earnest face. I realized he meant the words he had spoken, truly meant them. I was surprised. He didn't usually say anything like this to me. "Really?" I asked him, more curious about this turn of events than the school project we'd both soon be working on.

He nodded vigorously. "Yeah, sometimes I still feel so alone at the new school. I just wish I could see you. I didn't know you felt that way too." He unceremoniously plopped his armful on the table and hugged me.

I looked down at the top of his head, and suddenly I felt like crying more than I had all day. I furiously blinked back tears. The truth was, I wouldn't have minded if Mike were older and went to school with me. I think, even though it probably would've driven me crazy, I would have really liked to see his round mug in the hallways. Whether he was making a face at me or smiling, or even if he looked sad like me, it would've been nice. I hugged him tightly back.

"I'm sorry it's been hard for you too, little dude," I said quietly. Then, with a quick squeeze, I said, "OK, let's tackle this plant cell."

He looked up quizzically at me. "How did you know it was a cell?"

I glanced at the statue of Larry, who once again seemed on the verge of exploding with laughter. With a wave of his hand, he slipped off the counter, and I was left alone to deal with this.

It was a really good question. How did I know anything about the project, if not from a magical leprechaun--and, come to think of it, how did *he* know that? I looked quickly at the myriad of stuff on the table and said, "You think I don't know what a styrofoam ball is for when it comes to a school project?"

He thought again and said, "But how did you know it was a plant cell?"

Another really good question. This kid could be a journalist or a lawyer. "All the green stuff you have with you. Again, little dude, not my first rodeo," I said as I quickly surveyed the craft detritus covering the table. Mike looked at it too, and then back at me. There was a preponderance of green, but there were plenty of other colors as well. But he was more concerned about finishing than figuring out how I had become a Svengali.

We worked on it until nearly dinner time, which meant that it was boxed mac and cheese. I didn't honestly care. I wasn't very hungry, and I really didn't feel like preparing much. Mom didn't seem to mind either when she came home. As she gave Mike a hug, she looked at me quizzically over his head. Her eyes looked sad and kind, and I felt my own eyes well with tears. I gave a very small smile and shrugged, and she nodded.

During dinner, Mike regaled us with the intricacies of a plant cell. I was surprised at how much his tiny brain had absorbed from today's project. Although thinking back on it, I had only provided glue gun support and glitter control. He really had done most of it himself. Definitely a refreshing change from previous projects.

When he paused to take a bite, I spoke up, " Mom, can I ask you something?"

Mike almost looked relieved not to have to carry the conversation anymore, and he dug into the oddly fluorescent orange concoction with gusto. Mom smiled and shook her head at him, then turned to me, "Of course Mary-Claire, what's up?"

I swallowed, then said, "I think I need to be late coming home tomorrow after school. I hope I won't be too late, but I wanted to know if that would be ok."

Mom furrowed her brows and said, "I guess it would be ok. I might be able to come home a little early if I need to."

"I'm not a baby," Mike said unexpectedly, with mashed noodles and sauce spraying lightly out of his mouth as he spoke. Mom and I exchanged disgusted looks. "I can stay by myself if I need to. As long as I know about it."

Mom looked thoughtful for a moment and then looked at me, "It apparently won't be a problem, but why do you need to?"

I was prepared for this question, "I'm going to see that girl, Tessa, I told you about at the hospital. To see if there's anything I can do to help…or whatever."

Mom smiled now, a real smile, and said, "Oh, of course you can go, Mary-Claire! I'm so proud of you for wanting to. Mike and I can hold down the fort."

I returned the smile and then ducked my head. Getting praise for doing very little, while knowing the reason Tessa was there was because of me, was a bit hard to stomach. I excused myself soon after, with the excuse that I had a lot of homework.

I went upstairs and found Larry perched expectantly on my desk. He had a smile too, which unnerved me. Had he found a way to spy on me this afternoon? Did he know about me and Sean? I forced myself to look at him and smile. *Play nice, Mary-Claire, don't give anything away.*

"Yes," I said, as I opened a textbook a little roughly and forced him to move quickly out of the way. I was trying to buy a little time for myself.

"So," he said with a wicked grin, "you met with someone after school?"

"Yes, a teacher. Weren't you listening?" I said simply and then tried to focus on the textbook.

"I know when you're fibbing Mary-Claire," he said. He looked too happy, but unluckily for him, I had had time to craft a better answer. "You're right. I talked to Sean. He hates me. He heard me talking about the accident, and he told me to stop. That I didn't know what I was saying, and I needed to shut up. So, your little plan isn't going to work!"

I finished and sat down in a huff. I turned my head slightly so he couldn't see my self-satisfied smile. That lie was pretty good, and I was pretty proud of myself for thinking of it.

I heard him sigh heavily next to me. "Oh dear. This is not good at all, not at all. You do understand that I have to fulfill the wish you wished. What shall we do now?"

I looked over at him, and his discouragement was palpable. I kind of felt bad, but I wasn't going to help him. He'd made this mess for himself, and he was going to have to fix it without me.

~Chapter 12~

The next afternoon I skipped my final class of the day. Well, not exactly skipped. It was English, a subject I happened to be really good at, and since I'd read ahead in the syllabus and was a couple of weeks further than my classmates, my presence was not always required. I met Mrs. Montoya in the hall before class and asked if I could leave early because I had some important personal business to do. She quizzed me on the chapters we were reading for the day and, convinced that I understood them, let me go with a promise to be there tomorrow. Being a brown-nosing student can have its perks, I'm just saying.

The hospital was far enough away that walking wasn't an option. For the hundredth time, I wished that we had enough money for even a beater car. But I knew that it wasn't going to be a possibility for my entire high school career, so I caught a city bus to the hospital where Tessa was. I settled into a cracked red and white vinyl seat and checked my watch; it was almost three p.m. I had to make sure I was gone by four. This was not going to be a ploy to meet Sean. As I sat, I felt movement in my backpack next to me and looked down. Larry.

"And where will you be going, Mary-Claire?" he asked resignedly. He was wearing an old-fashioned nurse's cap, green, of course, with the normally red cross a brilliant gold. I hadn't actually seen him since yesterday. He really was a petulant little guy. Truthfully, I had hardly noticed. After talking with Sean, I really just thought about how to put my new plan into action. I was so focused on it that I hadn't had time to wonder why he wasn't around. I should've known that peace couldn't last.

I looked around the bus to see how close the next person was. Luckily for me, two o'clock in the afternoon is not a popular time to catch a bus. There was no one for several seats. Even so, I bent my head and pretended to rummage through my backpack. This was becoming my favorite ruse to keep people from thinking I was insane. Of course, now they were going to think I was perpetually disorganized, but with all my current drama, that hardly rated a second thought.

Although I suspected he already knew, I still answered his question. "I'm going to the hospital to see Tessa," I said quietly.

"Why," he said, with genuine confusion on his face. I was slowly beginning to understand that he really did not look at humans as emotional beings. In fact, I got the disconcerting and distinct feeling that he looked at us the way we look at animals.

I struggled to find the words to explain my reasons to him, but it was impossible because I didn't think he had enough of a conscience to understand.

"I just want to see her, that's all," I said.

"Are you checking on the competition, because I really don't think that's necessary," he said.

I couldn't tell if he was teasing or not, but either way, I thought it was in poor taste.

"I am not!" I said more loudly than I intended. I pulled my head up and looked around. I was definitely getting some weird looks for my trouble. I half smiled and then ducked my head back in my backpack.

Larry wrinkled his tiny forehead. He had not been kidding with his question. He sincerely couldn't figure out why I would go see her. He studied my face for several minutes, but I steadfastly refused to continue this conversation any further. And then he looked up with something akin to alarm in his eyes. "Did you say 'hospital'?"

"Of course I did. Where else do you think I would see her?"

"I don't like hospitals. They're creepy."

"Probably because you're afraid of meeting someone you put in there," I said bitterly, and he said nothing. In fact, he sat very still until we got to the hospital's stop. And then, "I'm sorry Mary-Claire, but this is where I take my leave of you. I shall see you when you get home."

And he was gone. I couldn't have been happier. It didn't even occur to me until I saw him in my backpack that I might have to endure seeing Tessa with Larry snarking on my shoulder. This was going to be hard enough without that happening.

I got off the bus and found myself standing outside the hospital entrance. My courage was failing me, and I wasn't sure about this anymore. But I had to, or at least I had to try. If the outcome wasn't positive, well, I guess I deserved whatever came my way.

Squaring my shoulders and taking a deep breath, I walked through the revolving doors. Once inside I quickly lost my nerve and lowered my head to look at the white tiled floor. I saw colorful arrows painted on the floor and figured they showed the way to different departments. The problem was I didn't know which department I needed.

I looked up and saw a large circular desk in the middle of the lobby. The woman behind the desk had snow-white hair piled in a messy bun on her head and round glasses over her incredibly bright blue eyes. She was pleasantly plump, a description I had read about before but never actually seen in the wild, and she was wearing a crisp white button-down shirt with a red cardigan with white polka dots and white trim. She looked like Mrs. Claus, at least how I had pictured her looking. Somehow, the idea of another mythical persona suddenly made everything easier. I drew a breath in and walked up to the desk.

"Hello. I'm here to see Tessa Austin, please."

She looked up at me and smiled. "Well, hello, dear. You are so polite. Are you family?"

I decided that lying was the best way forward here. "Yes, cousins."

She looked at me for a moment and then nodded, apparently satisfied. "The eyes. Your family all have the same eyes. Second floor, room 214. You're lucky. Visiting hours have just begun."

Her eyes crinkled in the corners when she smiled, and I had the absurd feeling that this hospital was filled with the otherworldly and I pictured fairies and sprites secretly taking care of the patients in the middle of the night. It was somewhat comforting, although my stupid mind instantly added ghosts and zombies to the list with Mrs. Claus and fairies. Man, having a leprechaun as a companion can wreak havoc with your mind.

I eschewed the quick elevator for a slower climb up the stairs. I wasn't in any hurry to get up there now, although a glance at my watch told me that time did not actually stand still, even in a preternatural hospital. I didn't know what to expect when I got to her floor. I wasn't even sure who to ask. But I hoped someone would be there to give me some guidance and possibly a chore I could do for Tessa. I both wanted and dreaded the idea of that person being one of her parents. I wanted their permission, but I wasn't sure I could look them in the eye, knowing that I was, in part, responsible for their daughter's condition.

As I came onto the floor and found the wing that housed room 214, my fears and hopes were crushed together. A handsome, dark-haired man who possessed a more than passing resemblance to Tessa was standing outside room 214, talking to a nurse. My bravado was definitely waning now, and I almost walked right past him. But then I caught sight of Tessa, her dark hair plaited in tight braids on either side of her head, her tawny skin looking pale, and tubes coming out of her, hooked up to so many different machines that my heart dropped. My fault, all my fault.

Mr. Austin finished talking to the nurse and was about to go back inside the room when I stopped in front of him. He looked at me, and I decided to see what my brain came up with.

"Uh, Mr. Austin?" I asked, my voice sounding dry. He nodded, waving off a nurse who seemed about to shoo me away. I swallowed, although there was no saliva in my mouth, and continued, "My name is Mary-Claire McColl." Good start, brain!

He looked down at me for a moment, a wary, puzzled expression on his face; I guessed he was waiting to see what else I had to say. The problem was I had nothing else, and my mouth felt too dry to speak anymore. Finally, after giving me a few minutes to end this awkward stalemate, he said gently, "Yes?"

I swallowed another painfully dry swallow and took a deep breath. "I go to school with Tessa," I said, carefully avoiding lies. I couldn't tell him the truth, but the man had been through enough without me lying to his face, whether or not he ever found out.

He smiled sadly at me, obviously still confused by my presence, and said, "How nice of you to come."

My guilt pounded in my head as I looked into his kind brown eyes. "I...I was wondering if I could do something for Tessa. I don't really know what, but I was wondering if there was *something* I could do for her."

He looked surprised at first, then tears filled his eyes. "Oh, that's so amazing. What a caring girl you are. Actually, yes, there is something that you could do if you would be willing." He looked through the glass at his impossibly still daughter. A tear rolled down his cheek, but he didn't bother to brush it away. "The doctors say that she's still in there, somewhere. And she can hear us. They say it could possibly be helpful if someone were to read to her."

I wasn't sure what I expected, but this was actually wonderful to hear. I could do something for her. I could find some way, however infinitesimally small, to make up for what I had done. The pounding in my head subsided for a little while.

"Her boyfriend, Sean, has been coming at four to talk to her. He's a nice boy, but I'm not sure how much longer he'll be able or willing," he said, his voice dropping, "to come. Not that I will blame him, but I know he won't hold on forever. Could you take over for him when he has to go to practice?"

His eyes looked so hopeful and happy that I knew I had no choice but to say yes. I knew I was going to have to clear this with my mom and drop out of the French Club, no big loss there, but it would have to work. Plus, if I was taking over for Sean, that would mean that I wouldn't see him at all.

I got home earlier than I had planned. Mike looked up from his game when I walked in.

"I've done all my homework. It's on the counter if you want to look it over," he said, actually turning off his game. I looked at him, and he smiled slightly. "I remember you said you were going to the hospital. I don't remember exactly why, but I thought that maybe you would be sad when you got home."

I felt tears welling in my eyes. It was so impossibly sweet of him. "Thanks, Mike. It wasn't the best, but I'm okay." He smiled at me and then went back to gaming. Then, he seemed to think the better of it, turned off his game, and looked earnestly at me. "So why did you go?"

I didn't think I wanted to talk about it, but suddenly I found myself eager to tell someone. I sat on the couch and told Mike about seeing the accident--leaving out the part of my leprechaun friend--and how awful school had been. I told him how I wanted to do something to help. Then I told him about Mrs. Claus at the desk, and he laughed. I finished with my new schedule, and he nodded. "OK, so I'll be on my own then. Cool."

I was shocked, but less so than I would have been a few weeks ago. We hadn't gotten along this well in months. Maybe years. "Thanks, little dude. Hopefully, mom will agree."

He smiled, "Don't worry about it. I can convince her. And I promise I'll be good and do my homework and not eat too much."

I grinned and was about to say something back, but then I caught sight of a flash of green and realized there was another conversation I needed to have. "Thanks again. I need to put my stuff in my room, and then I'll figure out dinner."

I stood and turned to go upstairs. I heard Mike turn his game on and realized the moment was gone. I was nearly on the second floor when I heard a faint, "Hot dogs. Let's just do hot dogs. And tots."

When I walked into my room, I was still smiling. Larry was sitting on the dresser. He didn't look happy or sad—he just looked. "So Mary-Claire, did you get all that guilt out of your system?"

My smile faded. "No. No, I didn't, and I don't think one visit will do it."

Larry shook his head, "I dinna actually think so, but I had hoped. This will make things harder."

I looked at him. "I told you. I'm done with Sean. I'm going to help the Austins with Tessa, but that has nothing to do with Sean."

"I'm sorry my dear, but it simply has to have something to do with getting with Sean. Because, as I keep telling you, I canNOT leave until you do."

I sighed. "We're going to have to figure things out. Because that's not going to happen."

Larry sighed, too, "There's nothing to figure out. Dearie, what are we going to do?"

"Well, *I'm* going to start going to the hospital on the reg. The rest is up to you."

As I dropped my backpack on my bed and started out the door, I heard Larry say wearily, "It always is."

~Chapter 13~

Football practice began the next week; with semi-finals around the corner, there was only so much time they could take off, tragedy or not. So, I started my penance. I went every day after school to read to Tessa from four to five. My mom protested the amount at first, but Mike was remarkably good at arguing his case. I think we both expected that he would be good on his own for a day or two, but then he would stop doing his homework and just play games and eat junk. We were, thankfully, quite wrong. He did his homework, he actually seemed to eat less than when I took care of him, and he never left the door unlocked. After week two, my mom quit worrying, and so did I.

This was good for me mentally because, in the first few weeks, I had to confess, I mainly went out of guilt. So much guilt that each word I spoke out loud felt like I was swallowing cinnamon. It was all I could do to stay for the full hour, but then, the next day, I would be there in ready anticipation of the slow torture to come.

But then, without even noticing, after several weeks of reading, I found myself entering the hospital with a spring in my step. I liked going. For one, Larry never came. Not once did he accompany me to see her. I would like to think it was guilt, but I doubt he had enough humanity in him to feel such a thing. No, I think he just really didn't like hospitals and, being a magical creature, never needed one himself. Anyway, that right there would have been enough reason to go, even if I hadn't started enjoying it.

But I did enjoy it. Well, I don't know if "enjoy" was quite the right word, but I certainly wasn't dreading it. I read what we were studying in English to her. At first, it felt like a little bit of a cheat since it was helping me too, but then, I felt like it was helping in more than one way. I was providing some entertainment to her, and I was, in a very small way, helping her stay caught up with school. I realized the ridiculousness of this thought, but I liked the idea of it anyway.

Every day I would pass Mrs. Claus and feel…safe. I actually knew she had a real name, but I liked thinking of her as a mystical persona guarding over Tessa and me, keeping out all that's bad, *Larry*, and surrounding the place with goodwill. It was one of my favorite things about coming to the hospital. Most days. But then there were the days when she would smile at me and effusively compliment my character. I had a much harder time with those days. I never felt like I deserved any praise for what I was doing.

One day I arrived in a particularly morose mood. Larry had been hammering me to befriend Sean. He just wasn't going to believe my protests that it was never going to happen. And his mercurial moods about the subject were starting to get old. Sometimes he would laugh and tell me that he knew I would eventually give in. Other times, like today, he would get angry and remind me that I would have him with me forever if I didn't change my mind. On days like that, I was happy to leave him at the revolving doors, but then I would feel doubly guilty that my good deed seemed to be doing me more favors than Tessa.

There were a couple of older ladies at the information desk when I walked past. I was grateful for this because I thought that Mrs. Claus wouldn't notice me. No such luck. Even as one of the women was gesticulating wildly about whatever it was she needed, Mrs. Claus waved and smiled at me, her summer-sky blue eyes sparkling in the sunlight, "Good afternoon Mary-Claire, what an amazing friend you are." Then she turned her attention back to the visitors.

There, she had to start the guilt before I even ran into Mr. Austin. That was a part of the routine too. He stood outside her door every day, waiting for me. At first, I thought he was checking up on me, but all he ever did was give me a progress report – nothing to tell ever – and ask what "we" were reading today. I came to understand that this was his way of making the horrible situation normal. And that would've been fine, but before he left, he almost always acted like I was something amazing, even though I knew so much better. I could put up with it because it was only for the last few seconds of our daily interaction. Then, always with one last sad glance at his still daughter, he'd leave me alone with Tessa, something which I appreciated and only later came to realize that it was probably a nice break for him. But I didn't need anyone else acting like I was some hero. Always, no matter how much I liked it, I remembered why I was there and what I had done.

I just wanted to get into the room with Tessa, but sometimes reaching her felt like running a gauntlet. I turned from my reverie about Mr. Austin and looked at the sweet lady at the desk who just wanted to compliment me. Part of my penance was taking the praise I hadn't earned.

"Thank you. I'm just doing what anyone else would do," I said, mostly to myself, my cheeks turning the color of my hair.

But, of course, Mrs. Claus had the enhanced hearing that only a supernatural creature could have. While the women were still trying to get their point across, she shushed them sharply, looked at me, and said, "Oh, Mary-Claire, if only that were true...this would be a lot happier place to work."

The women took a definite affront to the shushing and her attention to me. They started talking at a greater volume, with even more arm waving. Mrs. Claus snuck in a grim smile and wink before turning her full attention back to them.

I jumped into the elevator and gratefully watched the doors shut. One more obstacle and I would be in with Tessa, reading a Jane Austen novel to her. We were reading that in English, and I still fervently believed that if I kept her up with her reading if, not if– when, she was able to come back to school, she would not be too far behind. The only thing was, she would not be coming back to school, not any time soon. I tried not to let that pesky little thought bother me for too long.

I got off the elevator on the now familiar floor and immediately saw a short, plump blonde woman outside Tessa's door. I flinched and wondered where Mr. Austin was, hoping maybe he might finally trust me and not always be there when I arrived. Other than the praise, I liked seeing him and hearing about Tessa – oh, that there would ever be something positive to report – but I hoped he would eventually trust me to keep my word and my schedule. I hoped that mostly for him so that he might have a moment to relax and know that someone else would help take care of his baby. My routine had been the same for weeks, and all the nurses on the floor knew it too. They might greet me from time to time, but mostly I was left alone for my visits. To now have this stranger standing outside her door felt odd, almost wrong. I briefly thought she might be a new nurse, but I noticed she wasn't wearing scrubs, so I figured that wasn't the case. I had no earthly idea who she was, and I felt some trepidation as I walked forward.

As always in my life, when I needed some distraction, the floor seemed unusually quiet, and all I heard was the slapping sound of my shoes hitting the tile sharply. Apparently, so did the woman because she turned to me as I got closer. "Mary-Claire," she said timidly, questioningly.

"Yes," I said, wondering what fresh torment was coming my way. For a half second, I wondered if she was a detective investigating what they now knew not to be an accident.

"I'm Patty Austin, Tessa's mom."

I looked at her, confused. Of course, I knew Tessa had a mother, but she had never been there before. It was always Dennis. She looked nothing like her daughter except her eyes. One of the most striking things about Tessa was her deep green eyes, and I looked into the same pair now—the green eyes that had gotten me in to see Tessa on the first day. Her eyes were filled with sorrow and gratitude; mine were the eyes of a liar.

"Oh," I managed to say, sounding intelligent as always. I know I have a brain tucked somewhere in my head, but sometimes I think it's just a stem.

"I wanted to meet the girl who's been coming every day to read to Tess. Dennis has told me so much about you, and I just wanted you to know..." her voice broke. Tears flooded her eyes, and she wiped them away as she went on, "I wanted you to know how much what you've been doing has meant to us. Tessa's the oldest of five; I have two boys and two girls at home. I can't be here as much as I would like, and neither can Dennis. He has to work, and I can't leave the kids alone all the time. It's so nice to know that someone else is helping us take care of her."

The speech was too much. I almost blurted out the entire story, from my crush on Sean to finding a leprechaun to finding out the leprechaun was a demon. Fortunately, my brain stem kicked in and stopped me before I did. Wouldn't that just add salt to her wound? But because the story was the only thing in my brain, I didn't know what to say. In fact, I couldn't work my mouth even if I had tried. But Patty seemed overcome as well, and she just hugged me tight and then reluctantly let go. "I guess I'd better let you see her."

She started to walk away, and something about her gait told me she didn't really want to go. I watched for just a second and then decided to go with my instinct. "Patty, do you want to join us?"

It sounded ridiculous, and I cursed myself silently. Who the heck was I to ask a mother if she wanted to sit with her daughter? But then I saw her turn and smile. "I wasn't sure if you liked being here alone. Dennis says you seem anxious to leave when he comes back after your hour is up. But yes, I'd like that a lot." I smiled at her and then opened the door to Tessa's room.

"Hi, Tessa," I said brightly, opening the blinds a little more, as I always did. I didn't know if the nurses liked me doing that or not, but Tessa's face always looked less sallow when the sunlight was on it. Her dark hair had less luster in its tight braids, but she still looked lovely. I felt somewhat self-conscious with Patty there, but she looked so happy that I decided to just go with my regular routine.

"Just to catch you up, we finished Lord of the Flies a few weeks ago. That made for some pleasant reading, as you can imagine. We've started our Shakespeare segment. We finished Romeo and Juliet last week and have started Othello. Tessa liked the romance of R & J, but I think she really likes the intrigue of Othello. I mean, who doesn't love a villain?' I said as I settled myself in the not-so-comfortable pleather hospital chair on the left side of the bed. "It's slow going sometimes because Tessa doesn't always know what the words mean as I'm reading. So we look them up. For Tessa. Because I obviously know all that. I'm just kind that way."

I had gotten over the oddity of having someone in the room with me and was just concentrating on Tessa. When I first started coming, my interactions with her were stilted, and I felt awkward. I would come in and pull out whatever book I had brought and just start reading. And I read quickly and dully. I don't think I actually provided much entertainment for her. But then I got over myself, got over worrying about what other people thought, and I just started talking to her. I would start by discussing a little about my day; I would tell her a funny story or two from school. And I would for sure talk about the reading assignment with her. I didn't want her to be confused from book to book to play. Sometimes she didn't always understand a plot point, or get the inference, so we would research it together on my phone. I found her very useful.

"Now, where were we...oh wait! I forgot to tell you. Do you remember the horribly soggy potato tot things they serve in the cafeteria? You might not, you take much better care of yourself than I do. Well, anyway, Nate Campello wanted to take some to class like in that movie. So, he filled all the pockets of his cargo pants, and I mean all of them, with tots. But you know how soggy they always look? I've always assumed they were baked and just looked that way because they weren't fried. Nope! I don't know how the lunch ladies manage to serve them so mushy because judging by the grease oozing down his pant legs as he leaves, they are definitely fried..."

"Oh, my goodness, didn't he notice?"

I looked up in shock. I was so used to my time with Tessa and so into my routine that I had forgotten about my surroundings. And no one usually interrupts my sessions. I looked into Patty's eager face, grinned at her, and then looked back at Tessa. "Well, not at first, but he did eventually. Not only were they fried, but apparently freshly fried," I said, starting to laugh already. "It took about a minute, but then all of a sudden, he started yelling and dropped his pants to the ground. His legs were so red! Honestly, I think everything needs to come with warning labels."

I looked up from the bed and saw Patty giggling. I leaned forward to Tessa and said conspiratorially, "I don't know if I should tell you this in front of your mom, but Nate's been working out. It wasn't that bad of a sight, if you know what I mean." Patty's eyes got big, and she put her hand in front of her mouth to stifle her laughter. "Now that that's out of the way, we'd better find out what Iago's been doing. He's a sly one."

Patty sat with us for about twenty minutes. She seemed to remember her high school Shakespeare because she added some really helpful comments. It startled both of us when her phone buzzed, and she jumped up after checking a text. "I'm needed at home. I'm so sorry. I'd love to stay. This has actually been fun. Maybe we can do this again?"

I stopped reading and looked at her. I was surprised at the hope gleaming in her eyes. I smiled and nodded enthusiastically, "I'd really like that."

She nodded at me, tears glistening at the corners of her eyes. "See you again soon Mary-Claire," and then she was gone.

I had to look down quickly. A tear splashed onto the page. In all the weeks I had been coming, this was by far my favorite day. I didn't feel as guilty as usual. Tessa's mom had made me feel like I was making a positive difference.

I sat for a moment composing myself. Shakespeare is hard enough to read when I wasn't all choked up. I glanced at my watch and saw that it was four-thirty. I still had plenty of time.

"Right, that was fun, but now that it's just you and me, let's get back to Venice."

~Chapter 14~

     I meant to keep an eye on my watch as I read. I knew I only had a half hour until other possible visitors came. Sean was no longer coming every day, but that only seemed to make it more important for me to get out. I never knew if he was coming or not, and I was not anxious to run into him again. I had seen him a few times at school, and he actually came up and talked to me a couple of times, but that was it. Larry had been so excited the first time Sean had said anything. He hummed most of the day, which was really irritating, and not just to me. Everyone else could apparently hear him, but no one could figure out where the sound was coming from; Larry could throw his voice quite well. I heard rumors of musical ghosts over the next few days, which I personally found hilarious.

     After the first couple of times Sean talked to me, though, Larry started getting angry. He seemed to be realizing what I had been telling him from the day of the accident was true. I wasn't going to make a play for Sean. Quite a few girls, including some of the cheerleaders, had been making subtle attempts at him, but I refused. Brenna was definitely on the top of that list. I rarely saw him without her. I also rarely saw her at the hospital, so I was beginning to wonder at the depth of her friendship with Tessa. Charlotte was around him a lot too, but she was never hanging on to his words; I saw her at the hospital once in a while, usually when I was leaving, so I tried to stay off her radar by slinking out a side door or going down a different hallway than the one that led directly outside. She had seen me a few times, ignored me, but then had actually come up and said hi and asked how Tessa was doing the last time. Even though I don't think anyone can possibly know my involvement, and I prayed no one knew my thoughts on Sean, I was always wary around Tessa's crowd. Again, though, just as I had to admit with Tessa, none of them seemed like terrible people. But I kept my distance, just in case, and out of guilt.

My complete apathy to getting into Sean's inner circle was a source of irritation between Larry and me. "Colleen, you simply have to get over this misguided aversion to Sean. If it makes you feel any better, I know this is not what you were thinking when you wished. Although, I don't think you were thinking of much besides Sean at the time," he said earlier today. "But, no matter how you feel now, once a wish has been made, it must be fulfilled. So...."

I had shaken my head at him for the hundredth time and said, "I told you, and you're just going to have to get it through your thick Irish skull. I'm not going for Sean. Not today. Not tomorrow. Not ever."

This angered Larry, and he had gone his separate way from me outside the hospital, glaring and muttering in retaliation. It was hilarious watching the tiny figure storm off. Even though I knew the evil that could lurk within, he was so small, and, as previously noted, all things small are cute. But as I watched him go, I wondered when it was going to get worse.

Having my constant companion mad at me was so uncomfortable that it was truly enjoyable to be at the hospital today, a place in which Larry had never set foot. In fact, today, as I did more often than I cared to admit, I wished I could stay longer, but twice recently, I had to duck down a stairwell to avoid running into Sean. So, after the last near meeting was far too close for comfort, I always left ten minutes early and avoided the whole conflict.

But now, as I checked my watch, I realized something that made a knot in my stomach. It showed the same time as it did right after Patty left, four-thirty. The thing is, I had read more than one act since she left. I looked around for a clock and saw Sean standing outside the door. Great. My battery died. Stupid watch.

"Well, Tessa, we'll have to pick up here next time. Hope you won't be in too much suspense." Tessa's eyes fluttered briefly underneath her eyelids. Normally this sort of thing made me happy; I just knew it meant she could hear me and had some possible understanding of what I was saying. Unfortunately, the thought that she was there, unable to react while I conversed with Sean did not make me feel better today.

I got up as he opened the door. "I'm just leaving," I said, trying to sidle my way out the door.

"Mary-Claire!" he said, smiling. "I didn't know it was you who was reading to her."

I smiled back and said nothing, still making for the door.

"Do you have to leave right now?"

"Um, yes," I said.

Before he could respond, a beeping noise came from one of the many machines hooked up to Tessa. A nurse came in, pushing past me, which had the unfortunate result of pushing me further into the room.

"It looks like her heart rate is elevated," she said, then frowned. She picked up Tessa's hand and checked her pulse rate against her watch. She frowned again. "I'm sorry kids, I don't know what's going on exactly, but I think it best if she has no more visitors right now."

I tried to slip out unnoticed, but the nurse called after me, "See you tomorrow then, Mary-Claire?"

I nodded and waved and left quickly, but Sean still followed me.

"Do you really have to go? Don't you have time for a snack in the cafeteria?"

The cafeteria? Still in the hospital? No Larry? Despite my best intentions, I smiled for real and said, "I guess I could spare a few minutes."

We rode the elevator in silence, although it was not awkward. It felt comfortable. When we got off on the first floor, we went to the cafeteria. I tried to get my wallet out, but Sean insisted it was on him. He ordered us some sodas and a couple of slices of pie, which didn't look nearly as dry as the cakes sitting next to them.

As we sat at the table, Sean asked, "So, how long have you been reading to Tess?"

Ah good, an easy question to start with. "A couple of months now."

He took a bite of pie, mulled over the answer, and then said, "So...right after the accident?"

I nodded, "Yeah, I don't have much to do after school right now, and I just wanted to help somehow."

Sean smiled broadly at me, and I reveled in it but only for a moment. It seemed too perfect, too staged, so I looked around the cafeteria for any sign of green. I knew I was paranoid, but I think that's par for the course when you have a supernatural being as a roommate. I didn't care that Larry grew more sullen and resentful day by day. I didn't listen to him anymore when he threatened new harm to someone else to speed things up. I was not going to let that miniature demon win. And I didn't want to encourage him in any way.

"Are you expecting someone?" Sean asked, pulling my attention back to the table.

"Um, no," I said, and, having nothing else I wanted to add, asked, "How often do you make it here?"

"Not as much as I should," Sean said. He frowned, "I mean, I have football and homework and some real things that keep me away, but I also know I could make it more if I wanted to."

I said nothing, and he added, "Geez, that makes me sound like a real jerk."

"No," I said. "Not really. I imagine it must be really hard for you to see her in that condition. I didn't know her as well before, so I don't have all the memories of what she was like before to cloud my vision now."

Sean looked at me gratefully. "You really seem to get people."

I blushed and looked down at my untouched pie. My stomach was churning, and I felt like I was betraying Tessa. And I liked the way Sean was looking at me.

"Well, I think it's easier to diagnose other people," I said, thinking of the myriad of things I could improve about myself.

"I guess, although I seemed to have missed that life lesson. I never understand what other people are doing. Like you for instance," he said.

I stopped chewing the piece of pie I had just eaten. That wasn't a hard thing to do. It tasted like sugared glue with a newspaper crust. I thought chewing it was the hard part, but it turned out that swallowing was the most difficult thing.

"Me," I said after I managed to get it down with a big swig of soda. "What do you mean?"

"I don't understand why you come, day after day. The Austins have told me that you never miss a day. Why?"

He was looking intently at me. I felt myself go red, and I couldn't think of anything to say for a minute. Why did I come?

Simple, guilt. But that was an answer I could not give. Finally, I said, "In the beginning, it was guilt. I mean, something like survivor's guilt. You know, I had seen it happen, and my life stayed the same, but nothing will ever be the same for Tessa. And so I came by to see what I could do. But, honestly, now, I really like it. I read to her, and I talk to her, and it's a good, calm part of my day. No matter what happens at school, no matter what's going on at home, it's peaceful in her room."

He mulled this over. I could almost see him mentally trying to fit what I said with his view of me. I must have passed some test because he looked at me with such glowing approval in his eyes that it was physically painful for me to see.

"That's really incredible. And puts the rest of us to shame."

"Oh, don't think too much of me. Like I said, I like it, and it's an oasis for me. Plus, I read our English Lit books to her, so really, as I'm supposedly serving her, I'm really helping myself. See, totally selfish."

He laughed and placed his hand gently on mine. "I sincerely doubt anybody would look at you and think selfish."

I had trouble breathing. His hand covering mine felt warm and strong and so right. He was looking directly into my eyes, and I felt a sort of melty feeling. Crap!

"I have to go," I said as I abruptly got up and grabbed my backpack. "My little brother is home alone. I promised my mom I wouldn't stay too late."

"Can we..." Sean began, and I was afraid of the words that would follow. Luckily a busser dropped a whole tray of glasses just then, and whatever he was going to finish with got drowned out in the ensuing ruckus.

I waved goodbye and ducked quickly out of a side door, which caused me to get lost in the hospital for fifteen minutes before I found the exit.

~Chapter 15~

Thanks to my impromptu date—holy cow, was it really a date? —I got home much later than usual and found the door unlocked and Mike sitting at the kitchen counter drumming his fingers on the counter. I wanted to greet him with a smile, but I found myself in a state of electric irritation, and somehow, my little brother, with whom I had been getting along so well, was definitely a sparking point. Sadly, he looked particularly happy to see me, and this further amped the voltage. I stood in the entryway between the kitchen and hall and tried to ignore the happy puppy look he was giving and the incessant sound of his fingernails clicking as they hit the tile. The look was easy to avoid, but the sound of those nails clicking was grating. We stood at an impasse, me actively ignoring him, him actively attempting to make eye contact. And the clicking, that infernal clicking. Then he stopped, and I thought I'd won. I entered more fully into the kitchen.

Apparently, he took that as a sign that he'd won.

"Hey Mary-Claire, I'm hungry, and I don't want any of the snacks we have. Could you make me a quesadilla?" he said as I threw my backpack on a chair. Somehow, that was it. That was the metal that unleashed the energy in me. I turned on him with more ferocity than was, strictly speaking, necessary.

"Oh, for heaven's sake! Learn how to cook! It's not that hard," I said, throwing open the cupboard door, where we kept the frying pans, with such force that I heard a small crack and saw it slightly sagging on its hinges. Oops. But that didn't quell my fury. "And to lock a door!" And with that, the energy was spent. I contemplated the cracked cabinet door. This wasn't good. In my back-to-normal emotional state, I wondered how in the world I was going to explain this to my mom without her killing me or institutionalizing me. Both were viable and understandable options. Then, as I tried to decide my most likely fate, I remembered there was a witness to the event. I turned from the cabinets to my brother, feeling like a monster.

For his part, Mike seemed mostly just surprised at my anger. He sat blinking at me, not moving at all. I had really shocked him. Fair enough. I was late coming home, and normally I would have made him a snack just to keep him quiet, and I would have never mentioned the unlocked door because his being alone for so long was my fault. In this situation, which had played out countless times before, I was always the groveller, never the aggressor. He sat silent for a few more minutes, eyeing me cautiously and probably contemplating the least contentious move. I gave him nothing to work with, so he finally sighed and then asked, "Are you OK?"

I looked at him curiously, wondering how much he understood. I never thought him capable of deep contemplation of human emotions. I was grateful for all his help with getting Mom on my side, but I didn't think he truly grasped what was at stake. I had assumed he just wanted to be alone. Either he ran deeper than I thought, a slight possibility, or, far more likely, I was wobbling heavily on the edge of a mental crevasse. Could he see I was at the breaking point? I was about to answer him honestly when I saw the dreaded Kelly-green flash behind the canisters. I sighed deeply. There was no time for brother/sister bonding now.

"I'm OK, Mike. Just a long day, and I got lost in the hospital." I thought that if he was gaining more empathy, this answer was going to sound weak and pathetic. I had given him too much credit. Mike shook his head and snickered, then left the kitchen for electronics unknown. A few seconds after he left, electronic beeps echoed hollowly from the living room.

I watched him go and frowned. I actually would have loved to talk to Mike. The bond we were forming was really nice, and I wanted to keep it going. And the other form of life in the kitchen was the one I wanted to avoid. I studiously ignored the ruddy face I saw peering around the sugar and opened the fridge to see what we had available for dinner. There was not much there. On an average day, this would have frustrated me, and I would have gotten upset at my not-home-much-mother. Boy, I was really on one today; I should probably avoid poor Mom and Mike this evening. But today, it gave me a good excuse to stay buried in the cold for several minutes.

"Oh, come Mary-Claire, I can't be as bad as all that."

Unable to ignore him any longer, I raised my head above the edge of the fridge door and found myself eyeball to eyeball with

Larry. And strangely, his eyeballs did not look irate. Did they look...contrite?

"It's not you, it's me. I'm trying to think of something for dinner," I said, still not wanting a conversation with him. I ducked back down. Oddly, no groceries had materialized during our brief encounter.

"Of course, Colleen," he said, without the usual sarcasm. His entire attitude was off-putting as if some other leprechaun had taken over his body—a very nice and solicitous one, but it was weird having that coming from my little demon. It's weird how comfortable the familiar is.

"Mary-Claire, we have to talk. Something has to change," he said so matter-of-factly that I closed the fridge door and gave him my full attention.

"What's up?"

"My rainbow, without me dear, and I so desperately want to go home. But you have to understand that I cannot leave you without fulfilling three true wishes. At this rate, I'll not be home before you die. Can you not at least try?"

I pondered this question for a few minutes, more disturbed by his casual reference to my eventual death than I wanted to let on. "Do you mean with Sean? Because I'm sorry, I just can't." I wondered if my skin was reddening at this lie. On the one hand, I truly wasn't trying, but on the other hand, I think I was not stopping it as frequently and as effectively as I had before. And I did just have terrible pie with him. I ordered my mind to concentrate on the being in front of me.

"Do you really like me that much that you want me as a lifelong companion?" he asked, but this was no light-hearted banter. The near depression in his voice cut at me.

"You know it's not that," I said, a weak attempt at humor for which I was rewarded with a wan smile. "I just can't go for him after what happened to Tessa. Please, can't I just make another wish?"

"No, dear. That's not how it works. Once the wish has been said aloud, it's THE wish, until granted. We can't even move on to the next one. I told you that before. It hasn't changed," he said, his lilting voice sounding more mournful than cheerful.

"So, I can't wish for this cupboard door to be fixed," I said, attempting humor again and getting the same sad smile. "Honestly,

I'm sorry. But I can't like him now. I can't have what happened to Tessa always hanging over my head."

"What are we to do, Mary-Claire?" he asked, and his eyes pleaded with mine.

"Can I be his friend, would that do it?"

"No," came the answer, final and firm.

"Then I don't know what to do either. You should have thought of this before you played with her life."

His eyes took on the angry glint I had come to know and loathed, "You should have thought of that before you wished. I will get back to my rainbow."

The quick change in demeanor caught me a little off guard, but not much. His mercurial ways were part of his charm. There was a time it would have alarmed me, but not now, not for a while, actually. I realized as I looked at his angry little face that I no longer feared him. At least I no longer feared what he could or would do to me. I feared what he would do to anyone else he saw as getting in his way.

"Oh, go snag yourself a ride on another rainbow! I'm not going to play your game tonight," I whispered furiously at him.

He looked startled at me, the anger momentarily leaving his eyes and there was what looked like hurt, but the anger burned back in full force. "You'll play when I want you to," he said and disappeared.

I grasped the counter with both hands and breathed heavily until I calmed down. I don't think my small show of power was going to be a good idea in the end. I sighed and stared at the closed fridge door, running through recipes in my head to see what I could possibly make. It was then that I noticed the beeping and blasting from the other room had stopped. I frowned at nothing in particular. Had Mike heard my conversation? Had he heard Larry? Could he hear Larry? I wasn't sure if it would be better for Mike to hear me talking to myself or talking to an Irish man. Which would be easier to explain?

I shook my head in disgust at the mess my life was rapidly becoming. Well, there was one thing I could do. I picked up my phone and ordered pizza. Then I texted my mom and told her to pick it up. I knew this wouldn't thrill her, so I added some hasty lies about homework and headaches and a few truths about the hospital, and then I opened a book on the counter to set the stage.

Mom came home with the pizza but obviously was not very happy about it. She kind of snapped it on the counter. She looked at me, and I looked back innocently from my textbooks. I saw her form words, wanting to say something about me needing to do more, but then she sighed, grabbed a slice of pizza, and left the kitchen. Mike did the same, and I did too, but I went up to my bedroom instead of the family room. I didn't want to see any of her side looks right now. My angry leprechaun sidekick might actually be better than that!

~Chapter 16~

Oddly, I didn't see Larry the rest of the night and didn't enjoy it like I thought I would. I knew I had hurt and shocked him. I didn't mean to, I really didn't, but I had no idea what to do now. I wasn't going to let him fulfill the wish, so there had to be a workaround. There just had to be. These thoughts kept me up much later than I wanted, and I was groggy when I woke up. It was a nice surprise not to hear my mom crying. I looked at the clock to make sure I hadn't woken up late. I was actually up slightly before my alarm, which meant that she had not cried this morning. I hoped this would become a regular occurrence. Either that, or I hoped we would get a bigger house. Sometimes, hearing her sorrow in the morning makes it hard for me to get going.

Then I realized that Larry was not in my room. I showered quickly and got dressed. He was very good about giving me my privacy in the mornings, so I thought that once I dressed, he would appear. He didn't. Why was this so disconcerting? We had our share of squabbles recently, but he was never really far away. I packed my backpack, gave the room one more quick glance, and then headed downstairs.

Mom and Mike were already at the counter eating whatever they had scrounged up for breakfast. I greeted them distractedly. I think they greeted me back, but I wasn't actually listening. I looked for Larry all over the kitchen and even went briefly into the living room to see if he was there. And I did so while trying desperately not to seem as though I was searching for anything, and I didn't see him until I walked out the door. Then he was just there, standing in the walkway. I looked at the bus stop tiredly and realized that I was going to walk to school today. I knew we needed to talk, and I didn't think it would be possible to have the conversation on the bus. Well, it might've been possible, but I also didn't want any of the freshmen on the bus to start rumors about my insanity. I bent to pick him up, went to place him in my backpack, and thought the better of it. I tucked him on my shoulder and started towards the school.

He was quiet until we got away from most people, and then he said, "Well, thank you, Mary-Claire, it's quite nice to be in the sun today."

I looked around and saw no one, so I replied, "You're welcome. I'm sorry." I didn't give any specifics on why I was sorry because I didn't really know for which action or words I was apologizing. I sincerely meant my apology, but it was for everything and nothing all at once.

He was quiet for a moment and then said, "Thank you for that. I was just about to apologize meself. I dinna mean to imply last night that I was looking forward to you dying." He sounded really down, and I was shocked. I remembered the comment but hadn't been afraid, so I forgot it with all the rest that had been said.

"I wasn't afraid. I didn't think you would hurt me," I said matter-of-factly.

"Oh, lass, I would never hurt you. To be honest, I can't because I'm beholden to you, but also, I do like you. That's why I feel bad. I do not look forward to knowing you'll be out of this world. You are a bright spot. You are kind, and I'm having trouble working with that," he said.

"What does that mean?" I asked. I couldn't imagine how my being kind, if that were real, would be a bad thing.

"Well, usually, I do my thing, and then the human gets upset with me and pretends they hate the way I did it, but they go along to get what they want. You're not the first to wish for someone to be out of the way," he said. I felt him sit down on my shoulder. His voice sounded more normal now. He always seemed to like talking about his wish-granting.

"I didn't wish for Tessa to be out of the way!" I said more vehemently than I intended. I hated when he put it like that. I know I wished for Sean, but...oh crap. How exactly did I think that was going to happen? The truth was, I didn't think about it. I didn't think about anything but my desire. I was afraid of where this line of thought was going and forced myself to focus on Larry again, but his words were far from reassuring.

"You didn't aaanndd you really did. How did you think you'd be with Sean if Tessa was still there?"

"I didn't. I didn't think about anything," I admitted. I was defeated. I was a bad person.

"But that's the point where you differ from almost everyone else. See, I know now that you did not think about it, but you also did not want it the way I did it. And while all the humans eventually accepted it, I know you're having trouble getting over it. And that's my struggle. And yours."

Again, I hated this line of thinking. I could tell that he really meant what he said. But also, he still thought I would come around to his way of doing things. That I would voluntarily have Sean fall for me and fulfill my wish. I was just about to tell him once again how wrong he was when he said, "So that's what I'm working on. I'll see you later. Have a good day."

And with that, he was gone. Just gone. I found myself alone, which was a good thing because I had just gotten to the edge of campus, and there were starting to be more people.

I saw Brenna and Charlotte, but Sean wasn't with them. I didn't give in to the disappointment of not seeing him. I didn't want to see him anyway. I looked back at the girls and was surprised when Charlotte gave me a quick smile and wave. I guess we were bonding over the hospital? Brenna followed her gaze, and, oddly, even she gave me a wave and a nod. I couldn't figure out why, but Brenna said something to Charlotte, and she nodded, smiled and they moved into the classroom. I guessed then it had something to do with Tessa. I hoped neither of them would find out about Sean. If there was anything to find out. Which there wasn't.

The day passed in much the same rhythm. I was starting to interact more with people in my classes, so I had some distractions during the day. I was glad, was I glad, yes, I was glad that I had no classes with Sean, so I didn't have to rehash yesterday. The weird part was that I was unhappy that I had no leprechaun to run color commentary in my ear. He definitely seemed friendly this morning, and I liked him in those moods. I wondered how much longer they would last as time wore on. I felt pretty sure I would have a crazy cranky companion by the time I died. Finally, the school day ended, and I boarded the city bus to the hospital.

When I arrived, I tried to put any thoughts about the previous day out of my head. I didn't want to be thinking about Sean when I was with Tessa. That was out of the question but becoming increasingly harder to do. I waved distractedly to Mrs. Claus, and she waved back. She was on the phone, thankfully, so she didn't have time to interrogate me about the boy I got off the elevator with yesterday. I was sure she wanted to, but I scurried quickly through the waiting doors, and they closed before her call ended.

I went up the elevator, and when I got off, neither of the Austins appeared to be around. Good. At last, things were starting to go my way. Or had they been all day? Actually, I realized that today has been a pretty decent day so far. I slipped into the room, and Tessa looked the same. I hoped to see some change, but I guess it was better than getting worse. I dropped my bag by the bed and sat down. I began, as usual, by telling her about school. Really, not much had happened there today, but I found myself embellishing it to make it sound interesting. I finished by telling her that today had been pretty good. I told her I really hoped her day, in some way, had been as well. Then I read to her. We were both a little behind, so I mostly just read and didn't discuss too much. I finished the act we were supposed to have finished this week and looked at the clock. Just before 4, time to go.

"Bye, Tessa. Sorry, it was a rush job today. We've got to stay with the class, and I've been trying to explain to you what's going on so much that we've got behind. But we've caught up now, so I'll figure it out...I mean, I'll explain it tomorrow in more detail."

I left the room and looked around. No one else was around. I mean, the nurses were out and about, but they were all focused on other patients. The Austins still had not arrived. I hesitated in the doorway; I never really liked leaving her alone, but that was silly. She would be checked on soon, and I was sure one of her parents would arrive momentarily.

I got on the elevator, pushed the lobby button, and sagged against the wall. Now that I was alone, I played back my conversation with Larry in my mind. It felt off somehow. I wondered what he was planning, and I wondered how he'd take it when I didn't agree to whatever it was he had in mind. The floor pinged, and I decided it was a problem for another time. I got off and stopped to rearrange the folders and books in my backpack. One textbook, in particular, was pushing into my back, and I didn't need that the whole way home.

"Hi Mary-Claire," a voice said from behind me- a voice I knew well by now. I turned slowly and saw Sean in the corridor.

Inwardly, I groaned, but outwardly, I smiled broadly. Or did I smile inwardly too? "Hi Sean, what's up?" Good start; keep it casual.

"Got a minute for more pie?" he asked, smiling in return.

Dang, had he been waiting for me? Was I going to have to take the stairs from now on? I knew I absolutely could not be late two days in a row, so I promptly said, "Sure, who wouldn't have time for that deliciousness?"

He laughed. "Maybe we can try something else."

I laughed too, just to be polite, of course, and definitely not because the light in his eyes and the width of his smile were contagious. "Sadly, I think the pie was the best-looking thing there. There were some lumps of lard on cake, but I'm not feeling a heart attack today."

He laughed and looked me in the eyes, "Then maybe we should go somewhere else."

My brain shut off entirely. Going out of the hospital was out of the question for two glaring reasons. First, of course, was that it would be an official date and that was something I was studiously avoiding. Second, and certainly far less important, Larry existed outside these hallowed walls. I was safe here in my sanctuary; he didn't come in here. But if we ventured outside, Larry could be lurking under every bush and in every dark space. These were the thoughts running fast through my brain while I could feel my mouth breaking into a smile and possibly starting to form the word "yes."

But just then, before I could reply, I got a text from Mike. It said simply, "SOS, come home now. Mom needs us."

I couldn't fathom what would make him send that text, but all thoughts of an outside-the-hospital date with Sean fled instantly. Mike might exaggerate a lot of things, but he would never send a text like that unless it were truly urgent.

I looked up at Sean and saw him mirroring the anxious look on my face. "Is everything ok?"

I shook my head. "No, I'm needed at home. I'm sorry, but I've really got to go," And with that, I left, not getting lost in the hallways this time.

~Chapter 17~

I was just fast enough that I was able to catch my regular bus. I worried the whole way home. I wanted to text Mike for more information, but conversely, I didn't want to. I wasn't sure if I could handle bad news on a bus filled with strangers. So, I kept looking at my phone, willing him to text me and also begging him to not. The only thing that kept me somewhat sane was the idea that even Mike would know to text more details if it was something medically urgent. That gave me some comfort; she had to be physically ok. But what then?

When it was my stop, I jumped up from my seat and ran to the front. I think I pushed past some older people, but sadly, I didn't care. I wasn't really thinking of anything but Mom. I sprinted from the stop to our apartment complex. As I darted along the walkway, I suddenly wondered if Larry had anything to do with this. Hadn't he said that he was going to think of something? I didn't know how hurting Mom could possibly speed things along with Sean, but I felt like Larry wouldn't care. Burn the world down if it means Mary-Claire and Sean get together. The thought spurred me on the last few yards, and I burst through the door, thoroughly out of breath.

At first, there were no sounds, and I almost thought Mike had lied or exaggerated. I was just about to shout his name when I heard it. Quiet sobbing. Not overly loud, not exaggerated. If it hadn't been the afternoon, it wouldn't have even registered to me. It was the sound I had heard so many mornings. But never, ever, when she knew we were awake. And Mike had probably never heard it before because he only woke up when Mom insisted on it. I listened quietly as I did in the morning. And as always, I felt like I was intruding on her personal grief.

Mike must have heard me come home because he was bounding down the stairs two at a time. I watched him and thought he was going to miss a step and fall the rest of the way, but surprisingly, he landed somewhat gracefully and then turned to me. I looked at him, all the questions and fears jostling for space in my mind and not one brave enough to come to the forefront.

"Dad." One word, and though I felt relief that Larry wasn't behind this and hadn't done something reprehensible, the white-hot anger quickly pushed all other feelings aside. Dad. The person who had destroyed our home, the person who had left us all behind. Dad. He was the only one I could think of who would garner this reaction from Mom.

I started to go upstairs when Mike grabbed my arm. I turned, trying not to be too angry with him but wanting to get upstairs to comfort Mom. He had something in his hand. Something white and envelope-y. Something like a letter. No, the envelope was too big for just a letter. It was an announcement.

It was, to be exact, a photo announcement with four tastefully done pictures in black and white. There was a photo of a rose. A photo of two hands clasping each other over a protruding belly. A photo silhouette of a man and an obviously pregnant woman, facing each other, holding hands, foreheads together. And a photo, with one brightly colored pink rose laying at the base of a letterboard which spelled out "Baby McColl Coming this February."

I could still faintly hear the crying, but the rushing in my ears drowned out most other noise. Baby McColl. Baby Girl McColl. My dad, and the woman he decided was more important than any of us, was going to have another baby. A replacement family. That's why we never heard from him anymore. He didn't need us, he didn't need me, anymore.

I looked up at Mike, and he was shaking his head. "I don't know. She came home with it. He sent it to her office." He looked sad, a little haunted, and not nearly as angry as I thought was appropriate. Of course, he was the only one whom Dad hadn't completely replaced.

That thought snapped me out of my stupor. And then it hit me. Her office. He sent it to her office, to the people who would know the outlines of her personal story, but probably not many details. Coworkers who would be curious about the announcement, would wonder at the last name and think perhaps it was her brother. I had been missing my dad for so many months, praying for him to come back to put our family back together. Now I was glad that he was thousands of miles away, glad that my first wish had not been granted yet, because my second wish would carry twenty to life.

I squeezed Mike's shoulder, quickly thanked him for texting me, and darted up the stairs. I hesitated outside her room. I had never interrupted her sorrow before. I never felt like I should. But this was different. She had known Mike was home and couldn't hold it in until tomorrow morning. She needed me.

I knocked gently and opened her door before she responded. "Mom," I said and slowly walked in. She was sitting on the edge of her bed, head down and shoulders slumped. She didn't look up. I sat next to her and just laid my hand on her shoulder.

"I'm sorry Mary-Claire. I'll get myself together," she said, with one lone sniffle that managed to break me easier than her tears.

"It's okay, Mom," I said. "I just want you to know I'm here."

She nodded. "Thank you, love. I don't know why I'm such a mess. He's been gone for months. Almost a year. But this is…this is permanent." Now she shook her head, "I sound so stupid. It's been permanent for a long time."

I thought for a moment. "Yeah, I guess. But I'm angry too. And I haven't been for a while, but this is different."

She nodded again and then drew in a deep breath, then exhaled like she was expelling all the pain and anger. She did it one more time, drawing her breath so deeply I thought she might suck all the oxygen out of the room, then looked at me and smiled. She was slightly disheveled, but I'd be happy if I could look like my mom at her worst. "Well, I think I scared Mike enough for one day. What do you think?"

I smiled back but didn't look too deeply into her eyes. She deserved to keep something to herself today.

We went downstairs and found Mike sitting at the counter in the kitchen. He had his game open and was looking at it, but his fingers weren't moving, so he looked up right away when we walked in. Mike looked between the two of us to try and determine what the mood was. But, although his capacity for empathy seemed to be growing, he didn't seem to be able to read either one of us.

"Mom," he said tentatively. She rewarded him with one of her thousand-watt smiles, "Sorry, Mike. I didn't mean to scare you. The announcement was just a surprise, that's all. And I didn't handle it well."

He looked over at me to see if this all was true, and I smiled slightly and nodded. Then he looked at Mom and said with all the earnestness of an eleven-year-old, "Love you, Mom."

She looked shocked at the unprovoked announcement, not his normal modus operandi, but quickly hugged him. "Love you too kiddo. Thanks for calling the cavalry for me." At this, she beamed the same smile in my direction. "How would the two of you like to go out for dinner?"

Mike grinned like a maniac. "Really? Can we go to Peter Piper Pizza?"

I groaned and rolled my eyes, but Mike really deserved it tonight. So, I looked at Mom and nodded, and she looked at Mike and nodded.

We had a great time at dinner. We used to go out to eat a lot when Dad was with us, and this felt like new old times. It was comfortable, we laughed, and, truly, I didn't really miss my missing father. It wasn't a great feeling, but it was the truth. Time was starting to heal some wounds.

We got back pretty late, especially for a school night. I knew tomorrow would come soon, so I wished them both a good night and headed upstairs to my room. In all the excitement of the afternoon and evening, I had forgotten about my tiny companion. But as I ascended the stairs, I saw him standing at the top, in the middle of the hallway. He was smiling, which I found unnerving.

I looked around quickly but could hear my mom and Mike talking in the kitchen, so I felt safe.

"What are you so happy about?" I asked. He hummed softly, then said brightly, "I think I've worked it out. I know what we're going to do next with Sean."

I ducked my head and sighed loudly. The sigh was for cover, and the ducking was to hide my blush. I felt super guilty about the date I had enjoyed and just the normal guilt about how much I wanted to go on the one today, and yes, I was finally admitting it was a date. I also forgot, briefly, that Larry didn't go to the hospital and so didn't know about my meetings with Sean. And I felt guilty because, even without Larry's machinations, I was starting to fall for Sean. Well, I guess that was a given. But maybe he was falling for me.

"I don't want to do this right now!" I said much louder than I intended and then heard the shuffling on the stairs behind me. Oh, for crying out loud! I had also forgotten that I was standing on the stairs, staring –from Mike's point of view–at nothing and talking to the air. Mike wasn't saying anything, and I really didn't feel like doing this right now, either. I said nothing and just finished the journey to my room.

I shut the door much harder than I intended. Part of my thought process was that Mike might have wanted to come in and talk, and I was hoping to discourage that plan. But also, I was sick of Larry, sick of hiding how I felt, and sick of only talking to Sean in the confines of the hospital. It was both a sanctuary and a prison.

"Look," I hissed, "I don't want to talk about this tonight! I don't want to talk about it ever, but definitely not tonight! Just go away."

"Mary-Claire, you never want to talk about it," Larry began pleadingly, but I interrupted him. "No! Stop, for one night, for the love of all that is Holy, stop for one night!"

He looked at me, square in the eyes, angry and pleading and sad, "Fine, Mary-Claire, I'll let it go tonight. I'll leave ya to your keening, but we will talk. I'm up to 90 about this, and I won't be put off much longer."

He was gone in an instant. I didn't see where or how, but I knew I was alone. It felt good. It felt bad. I don't know! Tonight was the worst night in a very long time. I tumbled into bed and promptly fell into a fitful sleep.

~Chapter 18~

I woke up early the next morning to the sound of my mother crying again. I hadn't woken up early for a while, and I had almost convinced myself that she didn't do this every morning anymore. Just the sound wore me out; I admired my mother for starting every morning with heartbreak and then coming out ready to fight, showing the world she wasn't beaten. I just wish I had a little more of her in me. I was sad, and I didn't want to come out, fighting or otherwise.

I lay in bed, listening to her crying stop and the shower start. The sky was lightening, but I didn't want to get up yet. I hadn't seen Larry since the night before, but I knew I would have to pay for my outburst eventually. I just wanted to pay at home, in privacy. I was afraid that wasn't his plan. I looked lazily around the room, staring into every shaded corner, hoping for, and afraid to see, a familiar flash of green. Nothing.

After my mom's shower stopped, I reluctantly got out of bed and took my own slowly. The bathroom was still my greatest refuge. And the longer it took to find him, the more I worried about Larry's eventual return.

I stared at my soggy reflection in the mirror. The girl that stared back at me did not look thrilled. Or well rested. She looked tired, defeated, and frustrated. Well, too bad for her. The both of us were going to have to get used to a leprechaun for life. I was not going to complete the wish. And obviously, Sean would not either, once I stopped reciprocating, which I absolutely planned on doing the next time I saw him. No reciprocation. I looked back into the mirror and saw the girl with a light in her eyes. Dang it, even my reflection called me a liar when it came to Sean. I frowned at her and then left the bathroom. No Larry again. I sighed. It was going to be such a long day.

I got ready for the day methodically. I convinced myself that the reason I was taking such care with my hair and make-up was in case Larry chose to take his revenge at school. At least if I were revealed to be the school crazy person, I would look fantastic. I tried desperately to persuade myself that the thoughts of Sean flitting through my head had nothing to do with it. Nothing. I wasn't trying to attract him anymore, right?

There was a knock on the door. I jumped slightly but then shook my head and grinned at my reflection. Like Larry would knock. Or could knock. Even if he could, I doubted his tiny fists would make much noise.

"Come in," I said, applying the last swipe of the mascara wand.

My mom came in and sat on my bed. "How are you, Mary-Claire? With everything that's been happening, I forget to ask." She was staring at me intently. I wasn't sure if I liked the focus.

"Fine," I said cautiously. This whole scenario seemed a little odd, and I wasn't sure where we were headed.

"Everything is going okay at school," she continued, not smiling and never taking her eyes from my face.

"Yes," I said, completely confused now. Was school going okay? I had to admit it wasn't the highest priority of late. I assumed I was still doing well; none of my teachers had said anything to me. But had someone called?

"Are you sure?"

I didn't respond right away this time. What the heck was going on? Was I okay? Was I failing at a subject at school? Had someone noticed me talking to myself/Larry and told a counselor? I was trying to formulate a response that would be non-committal, give nothing away, and satisfy her. Nothing came to mind.

"Why?" I finally said, deciding to end the bizarre and uncomfortable game of 20 questions.

"Mike's worried about you, honey," she said, "And so am I."

That little worm! Just because I didn't make him a snack yesterday afternoon. Really, the kid is eleven; you think he would be able to slap some peanut butter on a cracker, for heaven's sake. Then, I took a deep breath and calmed myself down. Given how much help Mike had actually been recently, I knew his concern was real. Now I was worried about why he felt concerned. I prayed it was just my angry outburst with him a few days ago and not the conversation he heard on the stairs that caused his worry.

"I'm sorry I haven't been making him snacks and stuff. I've been late getting home from the hospital, that's all. I like cooking dinner and doing homework with him. I'll start doing better."

Mom smiled, but her eyes still looked worried. "It's not the snacks, sweetie. He's old enough to get himself a snack. It's that you were mad enough to break a cupboard door, yes, I noticed it, and he's pretty sure he heard you talking to yourself. Actually, he hears you talking to yourself a lot. He's worried."

I frowned. Well, dang it. I honestly thought I was exceptionally good at hiding it, and I thought Mike was really good at being oblivious. Was there a chance he was aware of life outside of gaming? That thought had never occurred to me. Of course, the thought that he might hear me speaking to Larry had not occurred to me either, so maybe I'm not the most introspective person ever. I just assumed Mike couldn't hear anything with his earbuds in and electronics absorbing his attention. I was struggling to come up with an easy answer to her worries.

"Do you think you should still be going to see Tessa every day?" my mom asked, and I looked up in alarm. I had not expected that response. Oh please, don't take the one thing I had going for me away.

"It was just a bad day, Mom! I am in high school. I like seeing Tessa. It relaxes me. It calms me when I'm stressed. There was something weird going on with her when I left. I was a little concerned, that's all," I said, the words coming out in a torrent.

"Okay, okay. I'm certainly not going to forbid you from going. But I just don't want you taking on too much. You should have a social life at your age."

The irony that the thing she wanted me to stop doing was the one thing that was giving me a social life was not lost on me. If she took away Tessa, I might not see Sean again. I stopped short. That thought was disturbing on so many levels.

"I'm doing good, Mom, really. I was just worried about Tessa, and I'm truly sorry about the door."

"It's alright, honey. Those are some cheap cabinets, that's for sure," she said, standing up and going to rumple my hair. She stopped, though, and looked at me carefully. "You got a hot date today? You look really good."

I looked at myself in the mirror over her shoulder. I had been so busy getting ready I hadn't really noticed the end result. I had done a small French braid across my forehead and tucked it in on the side, leaving my auburn curls softly cascading down my shoulders in a very becoming style. The golds and browns I had used on my eyes were making the green even more startling and quite beautiful. I had dusted my cheeks with a tawny blush and put a pinkish-brown color on my lips. It was a color I'd forgotten I owned, but the total effect was amazing. I looked good; false modesty aside, truthfully, I looked stunning. Looking at the girl in the mirror, I couldn't lie to myself anymore: I didn't do all this just in case Larry pulled something at school. I had done this for Sean.

I blushed and looked up at my mom. "Well, some days, a girl just wants to look her best, right?"

Mom genuinely smiled at me, "Some days, a girl does indeed. And some girls are lucky enough to look like you when they do."

She left the room, and I stared in the mirror. As it had become the norm lately, my brain stem seemed to work better than my actual brain. Maybe I should get ready more often while thinking of something else. I was going to look in my closet for an outfit when I noticed one laid out on the bed. It was a soft yellow T-shirt and a green and yellow floral skirt. A green patterned silk scarf that my mom had bought for me lay jauntily right by the neck of the shirt.

I had never worn the scarf, the petty side of me not wanting to because I was sure my mom had given it to me to up my sartorial game. Now, however, it seemed like the perfect complement to the outfit and my make-up. I tied it around my neck and instantly felt like a 70-year-old European. I frowned, then tied it around my hair, making sure to leave some curls loose. It really brought the whole thing together.

I was on a roll today. Just wait, I bet Sean's sick today. Despite my previous self-honesty, I didn't like the truth of how that thought disappointed me. So, while I could no longer pretend Larry had anything to do with how I looked, I decided to focus on feeling good about myself and, maybe, trying to meet some new people. In fact, I vowed I would avoid Sean at all costs. There, so I wasn't going to give in to Larry.

I got dressed and as I was leaving the room, I caught sight of the scarf in the mirror. The flash of green made me remember Larry, and I looked around the room for him. It had been a pleasant morning without him, but I was sure I was in for something today. My hopes of getting it over within the privacy of my home were dashed as I didn't see his tiny face anywhere.

"Dang," I said to myself, closing my door. I looked down the hall and saw my brother's worried face looking at me from his door. He closed it slowly, and I groaned. Yep, today was going to be something alright.

~Chapter 19~

Larry joined me at some point between leaving the house and arriving at school. I honestly believed he was some sort of leprechaun ninja. Lepra-ninja; that was the word I used for him in my mind. Anyway, I wished I knew how he had just appeared inside my backpack, in my room, and on my shoulder, as he had today. I was just sitting, minding my own darn business at the back of the bus, when all of a sudden, I felt a jolt on my shoulder and a small hand on my neck. You would think I would have gotten used to this at this point, but I have not. I startled and yelped, earning myself some quizzical looks from a couple of freshmen in the seats just in front of me. I glared at their turtle heads until they slipped back behind the green Naugahyde.

"Halloo Colleen. How's it goinnnn," Larry said, his voice sounding oddly...slurred? Even more strange was the backward green baseball cap, any guesses about the color of the buckle in the back? He looked like a charming, tiny gang member, although the charm was mostly because of his size and the ridiculous cap. Then my brain took in the full effect; was he drunk?

"Um, hi," I said, with my usual sly, side-mouthed whisper. Now that I knew Mike had seen me talking to Larry, I wondered if other people had noticed. I found that thought terrifying. I looked for the heads peeking above or around the seats, but no one seemed to have noticed. Or if they did, they were sufficiently scared of me not to bother. I probably should have been a little more cautious, but the high school was large, and the chance a random freshman would cause me issues seemed small.

"Todaysss the day bonnie lassssss," he said, and now I was sure he had imbibed something a little stronger than water, but I chose to ignore the obvious and prayed I was wrong. I patted his head, wondering how that would look to anyone who glanced my way. Hopefully, like I was scratching my shoulder. Hopefully.

He calmed down with the motion and snuggled into my neck. I thought I heard him snoring. I kept him asleep for the rest of the ride. If anyone was looking, I'm sure they thought I had some hideous rash. Is a rash worse than crazily talking to yourself on the scale of social suicide? What was the scale for crazy anyway? I wish I knew, and I was sure I would find out at some point. Larry wasn't going anywhere for the foreseeable future.

We got to school, and I mostly waited for everybody else to get off. Larry was still sleeping, and I didn't know how well he was able to balance when sleeping. I wasn't sure what my plan was if he fell off. On the crazy scale, would a weird tiny man falling from one's hair be worse than frantically trying to catch something no one else could see? It was a conundrum I did not want to figure out in real life. I walked slowly, putting both of my backpack straps on so that one nestled next to him, hopefully cementing his place. I smiled at the bus driver and then realized I must have been walking weirdly because instead of returning my smile, he just looked at me, looked oddly at my neck, and gave a half smile as he turned. Great.

The hallway was crowded with students trying desperately to get as much socialization in before the first bell rang. The jostling was sure to wake him up and this was not the place to attempt my new ventriloquist act. I looked around for an escape and noticed no lights on in the room to my left. I ducked into what was apparently the band room and pulled him roughly off my shoulder. He somewhat woke up and twirled shakily around the desktop on which I had deposited him. I couldn't ignore the obvious anymore.

"What the heck, Larry? Are you drunk?"

"Scuttered? Me? I harrrdleee think so," he said in his most stern slur as he stopped moving and tried desperately to focus on me. "I don toush the bevvies when I'm worrrkin," and for added emphasis, he burped loudly. "Honestly, I'm just a wee bit knackered."

I groaned deep within myself. "Go home, Larry, and sleep it off. Or just go to sleep, whatever. You can make my life miserable tomorrow."

Larry scrunched up his face and looked hurtfully toward the air in my general direction. "Och, lassie, do I make you sad? I dinna mean to. I'm going to help make you happy today, tha's for sure."

Heaven help me today, I thought desperately.

"Larry, I'm happy today. Really. See, don't I look happy?" I asked, smiling so big that Larry stumbled backward and fell off the desk. I reached quickly for him, but he was already clambering back on the desktop.

"Ohhhhhh, theressssss a feek! My gooooodnesss! You look like a right Beour, you do," Larry said, his eyes finally focusing blearily on me.

I shook my head impatiently. I didn't need this today. Well, really, who needs a drunk leprechaun any day? But I had been feeling pretty good about myself, and I had no idea if he was complimenting me or comparing me to a donkey's behind. What I have found is that when Larry gets his Irish on I need some sort of translator. I thought they spoke English in Ireland.

"Um, thank you," I said, assuming that "Beour" and "feek" were compliments; the words themselves were a mystery to me, but his voice sounded complimentary when he said them. "I think I can handle today by myself. Feel free to sleep this one off."

"Thank ye lasssss. I'm ssure a few zeds will hellllpp take the edge off," Larry said, and with that he disappeared, a lepra-ninja even when drunk.

I looked around the band room. Instrument cases were lying at odd angles all over the room. Music stands stood akimbo in front of metal folding chairs that were probably supposed to be in some order but weren't. I was sure it was the band teacher's nightmare. But it was Friday, and he had apparently given up. High school kids were the worst. Luckily, though chaotic, it appeared empty. I hadn't really checked to make sure no one was in here when I entered, rookie mistake. You'd think I had just gotten a magical companion instead of having him around for months. Fortunately, there was no one gawking at me as though I had grown another, albeit very small, head.

I caught sight of myself in the cymbals, and even in the fun-house reflection shown therein, I could see I still looked good. I smiled, something – I was quick to note – which made my face look slightly more becoming. Then I heard Sean in the hallway. The sound of his voice made my heart beat faster, brought color to my cheeks, and made my skin feel electric. I started almost drifting toward the door. Darn, I wasn't keeping my promise very well.

I opened the door cautiously. I wanted to stay in my refuge until the coast was clear, but I was vaguely more afraid of confronting one of the music teachers than I was of bumping into

Sean. I had no reason to be in the band room. I had no musical ability of which I was aware, and I'm pretty sure if any teacher saw me slinking out of the empty room before school started, I'd have some explaining to do. The problem was that my actual purpose was so patently ridiculous that I knew there was no way I could possibly tell anyone. I sucked in a long breath as I waited, but I saw no lurking teachers, so I slipped out and found myself directly behind Sean's group. They were walking boisterously, laughing and shouting at each other. In a stroke of incredibly good luck, I don't think anyone noticed me. I released the breath I'd been holding and watched them go for a minute. Wouldn't that be amazing to actually be a part of them? But I was holding firm to my vow.

I ducked my head and watched my feet as I made my way to my first class. I was afraid of seeing him, of him seeing me, of what I might not be able to keep off my face. I wasn't sure if the crowded high school hallway was the best place for us to discuss what happened at the hospital. Although, I thought to myself, what had actually happened at the hospital? Nothing really. Pie. And not even good pie.

Luckily for me, my feet knew the way to my first class without my brain. Actually, since Larry arrived, my entire body seemed to have found a way to work without a brain. Good for me. I had just arrived at the door when I felt a hand on my shoulder. I jumped slightly and turned, expecting to see a teacher. It wasn't.

"Hey, Mary-Claire. I thought I saw you," Sean said, smiling.

I smiled back, a mimicking reaction.

"Was your brother okay?"

"He was fine. It was a small family emergency, but all good now," I said brightly, trying desperately to keep my voice calm. Oddly, I didn't feel too weird, but just being this close made me a little breathless.

Sean looked concerned, "Are you sure everything is ok? I mean, 'emergency' sounds a little bad."

I mentally cursed my word choice and nodded my head, "No, yeah, I mean, that was a poor choice of words. My mom got news about a former family member, but then it turned out it wasn't really anything," I realized this still didn't clear things up, so I finished by throwing Mike under the bus, "My brother got a little over-excited.

It's really ok now." That was as close to the truth as I felt like getting in the school hallway.

"I was hoping we could have gone for another cafeteria date. I really enjoyed the first one," Sean said.

Did he use the word date? I chose to ignore it so I could keep talking without melting. "Yeah, me too, but duty called," I said lightly. When would the bell ring and save me?

"Would you like to get together today? After practice and the hospital? We could get ice cream," he said.

I wanted to say no. I definitely meant to say no. It was on the tip of my tongue when a soft "Sure" came out, as calm as you please.

Sean's smile grew. "Great. I know you have to watch your brother. Why don't we just go out after dinner? Or for dinner? Do you think we could just go out for dinner?" Even with my addled brain, I noticed he was talking fast and anxiously. What the heck? Was he nervous? And then my brain caught up with the conversation. I believed he was asking me for a date, an actual date.

I found this turn of events somewhat disconcerting. Had I really stumbled myself into a date? For sixteen years of my life, I've waited for someone to ask, and the one time I actually did not desire it—that's my story, and I'm sticking to it—was when it happened.

"Maybe, I'll have to check, but that sounds good," I said.

Sean graced me with one more magical smile and said, "Great, how about I pick you up at the hospital? You usually leave at 5, right? So, I can pick you up at 5." He started to leave and then called back, "You look really nice today. See you at 5!"

He was gone before I could think of anything to say. I watched the crowd swallow him up and wondered why my life was so out of control. I looked around for a flash of green, truly expecting a drunken leprechaun to be behind this strange turn of events, but I didn't see any sign of Larry. This was really happening. I didn't know how to stop it, and I didn't want to. Maybe my mom would help me out of this. I shot off a quick text asking if it was ok if I didn't come home from the hospital and went to dinner instead. I knew that my mom had some meetings today, which would naturally make her late coming home. Mike was certainly unable to care for himself, so I was pretty sure what the response would be, but I found myself disappointed. My mother didn't text back right away or even throughout the entire day. How was I going to find Sean and tell him I couldn't go if my mother didn't give me an out?

~Chapter 20~

I went to the hospital after school, but the pit in my stomach got worse as I entered. This place had become as familiar to me as my own home over the past few months. I took in the soothingly bland walls, the magazine rack with magazines I think had actually been there the first time I came, and the round plywood information desk with my favorite otherworldly creature sitting behind the desk. Her hair was a perfect height white chignon above her pretty, plump face. Mrs. Claus' eyes sparkled when she saw me. Some day I will learn her actual name, but for now, I reveled in the comfort of Santa's wife watching over me.

"Hello Mary-Claire, it must be four o'clock. You are a marvel of punctuality."

I smiled in return, swallowing the bile in the back of my throat. "Yeah, that's me. I..." I began, but my phone buzzed in my hand. "Oh, excuse me, it's my mom."

"A good friend and dutiful daughter," she said, beaming at me, then returning to her computer.

"Hi, Mom," I said, ducking into the elevator and pushing the second-floor button.

"Hi dear, I got your message," my mom said hurriedly.

Sensing that she didn't have much time, I said quickly, "It's ok, I understand. It's not that big a deal anyway. I'll come right home."

My mom laughed, "It's ok, sweetie. I don't have any appointments this afternoon, and Greg had an emergency at home, so they canceled our meetings. I can be home by five. You go ahead. Who are you going to dinner with?"

I was so shocked at my mom's answer that I didn't notice the elevator doors opening on Tessa's floor. The doors closed and the car had started its smooth ascent by the time I realized my mother was not saving me.

"Um, this boy. Sean. He goes to school with me," I said, watching the numbers climb to ten. A doctor got on and pushed the main floor button. I pushed two, and he looked at me oddly.

"Oh! That's wonderful. Go have a good time. I'll see you after dinner. Bye." I wasn't sure if I was more pleased that I was going to be able to keep my date or hurt at the amount of sheer surprise in my mother's voice. Or nauseous that I had a date with Sean. My emotions were all over the place. Once again, I didn't notice the elevator doors opening on the now familiar floor, but the doctor politely clearing his throat alerted me. I stepped off quickly and then just stood there. I didn't want to see Tessa today.

It took me a few minutes of psyching myself up to get my feet to move in the direction of Tessa's room. I paused again outside her doorway, but I knew that I needed to go in. I couldn't abandon her just because I was guilty. Heck, if I were going to do that, I wouldn't have come in the first place. Just add a little more guilt to the pile. No big deal.

I picked up the book lying on the stand by her bed. It was still Shakespeare's Othello. Today, the story of betrayal seemed a little too on the nose. I turned to where we had left off, Act III, Scene iii, and quickly realized that Iago was immersed in his betrayal of Othello, insinuating to him that Desdemona was unfaithful. Honestly, sometimes I think my life is being choreographed right now.

I looked at Tessa lying helpless in her bed and realized I had to cancel my date, but first, I had to confess to her. I don't know if she could hear me, but I needed to say the words.

"Tessa, people think I'm such a good friend to you, and you're probably in there wondering who I am and what I'm doing here. That's a story for another day. But I have to tell you, I've had a crush on Sean for a while. A long while. Before your...before you fell. I don't think he ever knew I existed, and I wasn't trying to steal him from you. I didn't start coming to see you because of him. In fact, I tried to avoid him. I haven't made any plays for him either. But he asked me to go to dinner with him tonight. I said yes, but I'm going to cancel. I'm sorry. I never wanted to hurt you. I just wanted to know what it would be like to know him. He's really nice, but it's not right. I'm sorry. I'm so sorry." The last five words came out in a sob. I wasn't just apologizing for Sean; I was apologizing for everything. For all the things I couldn't even say. I put my head down and cried into her mattress. I let guilt and the frustrations and loneliness of the past months flow out. And it felt freeing.

"Oh, Mary-Claire, you poor, sweet child," a voice said from behind me, and I jumped. I looked around and saw Patty standing at the door. Her plump face was creased into a smile as two tears slid down her cheeks. Her eyes, Tessa's eyes, held only compassion.

I wiped my eyes furiously. I didn't know what to say. I didn't know how much she had heard, and I didn't want to volunteer the information first. Patty came towards me, her arms outstretched. "Come here, honey."

I went to her and was enveloped in her embrace. The hug was sweet, comforting, and deep; I got the distinct impression that she was hugging her daughter by proxy, and I cried harder. She patted my hair and crooned my name softly, and I finally stopped crying. What a mess I was, if the mother of a coma victim felt the need to comfort me.

"Go on your date, Mary-Claire," Patty said when my sobs had subsided. I looked into her deep green eyes. Had she truly just said that?

"I never..." I began, but she smiled and said, "Sean's a great boy, and we liked him as her boyfriend. But honey, they are sixteen. Sixteen! They weren't married or engaged or even headed that way, most likely. And you are sixteen and a marvelous girl to boot. Go out with him, with my blessing. Tessa would give it to you, too, if she could. She's always more sedate after you come. She loves having you read to her. I know it. I just know it."

Tears started coursing down her cheeks now, and it was my turn to give a comforting hug. Had I really just gotten permission from Tessa's mother to go on my date? Could I actually go tonight and not feel guilty, well, any more guilty than I would have?

"I never meant for this to happen," I said.

"I know, dear, because if you did, you'd be terrible at planning. I've been here more than you know. I've seen you duck out right before he arrives—every single time, right before he arrives. I've watched you check the clock, always aware of the time. I'm not stupid."

I blushed and looked at the white tiled floor. "I...I've had a crush on him since we moved here, but..."

"Well, of course you did. He's one of the nice ones. And cute, too," Patty said, her eyes sparkling.

I bit my lip for a second, "Is it honestly okay? Because I swear, I won't go out with him if it upsets you. I don't want to give up coming in to see Tessa. It won't be worth it to me."

One large tear rolled down Patty's cheek as she drew in a deep breath. "Oh, Mary-Claire, I know you wouldn't. I know you were serious when you said you would cancel the date. And I don't want you to do that. Go, have a good time. Go to dinner, go to a movie. Go do what all sixteen-year-olds ought to be doing. That will make me most happy." There was real joy in her eyes, even as she looked at the still form of her daughter. "I would never deny you the right to be happy."

I smiled through the tears that had started down my cheeks again and felt all the guilt I'd been carrying leave my body. I felt almost weightless compared to the way I had felt walking in. Patty hugged me again until we both stopped crying. And then, with a squeeze of my arm, she let me go.

"Just one thing," Patty said, looking me square in the eyes, "Come tell me, come tell us about it on Monday."

I looked at Tessa and then at Patty. Tears welled up in the corners of my eyes again. How could this woman be any more wonderful?

"Do you want me to read to her?" I asked, uncomfortable with all the emotion in the room.

"No, let's just talk. I think she'd like that too. I talk to her all the time, but it's a one-sided conversation. I think she'd like to hear from someone else."

So, Patty and I sat and talked for the rest of my visit. It felt odd not to be reading to Tessa, but we talked to her too, and somehow, for the first time in ages, the guilt seemed to lift off of me. I wasn't a horrible person, and I hadn't wanted this. I could never have known what was going to happen when I made that wish. But I was doing what I could to make it better. And I had not tried to date Sean, but it was happening. Maybe I should just let it happen. But I would keep it from Larry as long as I could. He was going to have to stew a little longer.

~Chapter 21~

I left Tessa's room feeling better than I had since the day of the wish. Patty was amazing, and my biggest regret was not knowing Tessa before. With Patty as a mother, I don't think you could help but be a great person. I walked past Mrs. Claus on my way out the door and smiled at her. Maybe it was the first real smile I'd given her since I started coming to see Tessa.

She returned the smile and said, "Well, that must have been a good visit, my dear. You're positively beaming."

Before I could even nod my assent, she continued, "Or does it have something to do with that handsome young man who's been nervously amusing himself in the gift shop for nearly an hour?"

I stared at her and then craned my neck to see just beyond her into the gift shop. Sean was standing with his back to me, reading greeting cards from the rickety wire turnstile. He picked up one, seemed to laugh, and then replaced it and picked up the one next to it. I frowned. Just my luck, he seemed to like me, but only because he'd officially gone insane.

"How long has he been there?" I asked, still watching him. Thanks mainly to Patty, I was a little later than usual, but only by fifteen minutes.

"I'm not sure when he got here, Mary-Claire, but I noticed him almost an hour ago. He paced the lobby for a while, chatted me up for another while, and has been stalking the gift shop ever since." The corners of her eyes crinkled as her smile widened. "Old Bob wanted to call the police, thinks the boy is casing the joint," and at this, her too-blue eyes twinkled merrily, "You know, because hospital gift shops are huge with thieves and the like. But I told Bobby I've seen him plenty of times. So, he let it go for the time being."

I looked at the gift shop once again, mystified at the idea that Sean might be excited about a date with me. Even after all our interactions, it still seemed odd and incredible and... really, really nice.

"Go on, Mary-Claire, I think Bob's getting antsy again."

I looked at the gruff man behind the counter and smiled. If she was Mrs. Claus, the older man standing at the register was Father Time. His craggy face and gray patchy hair made him look like he'd been watching over the dusty stuffed animals and overpriced pieces of jewelry since the hospital was built. Perhaps they had built the hospital around him, thinking it was easier to incorporate the ancient human into the edifice than move him. In fact, with his withered expression, it was easy to imagine the whole dust-to-dust thing applying to him specifically. Father Time, Mrs. Claus, and somewhere in this world, a demented lonely leprechaun. And just for today, that thought did not depress me.

"I'll go rescue him," I said, and then my cheeks complained as my smile took over my whole face, "I don't want our first date to be bailing him out of jail."

I heard Mrs. Claus chuckling as I walked quickly towards Sean. Once I got close, though, I wondered what I was going to say. I never got as far as conversations when I daydreamed about him. I looked over at wizened Bob behind the counter and realized she hadn't been joking about him; he looked angry, and his mood didn't seem to improve upon seeing me.

"Um, Sean?" I said, tapping his shoulder. He jumped slightly, knocked into the cardholder, and sent a cascade of poorly held cards to the floor. Behind-the-counter-Bob made a growling noise, but Sean grinned at me as we bent to pick them up.

"I got here a little early," he said, with no trace of self-consciousness, and then he stage-whispered conspiratorially, "I think that guy's wondering what I'm doing."

I looked up and saw Bob grimace. I tried to keep my composure, but as I turned my attention to the cards and Sean again, I laughed and said, "Yeah, well, the information lady told me that he's been thinking about calling the cops, you know, 'cause you're planning a great heist."

Sean laughed, too, and said, "Right, I want to go to jail over overpriced candy." He looked into my eyes for a moment, then his smile deepened. "Should we get out of here? Hospital food might have been good enough for our first date, but I think I can do better for our second date."

First date? Second date?? What had happened? How did I get here? I didn't mean for this to happen. Hadn't I tried to stop it? Didn't I avoid him well enough? And yet, here I was going on my second — second? — date with Sean. I thought it was somewhat generous of him to call stale pie a date, but who was I to argue? These questions swirled around inside my head, and then I looked at him, saw his smile, and decided that it didn't matter what Larry had done, I was going to enjoy this night.

We quickly gathered the cards together. I heard Bob clearing his throat behind the counter. Even that sounded dusty and old. I chanced a look up at him, and his colorless eyes stared at me. He didn't smile, although, up this close, I wasn't sure his skin could crease into a smile without breaking apart entirely. That vision didn't help things as I then imagined his skeletal face still angrily watching me. I ducked my head again and found myself face-to-face with Sean.

"He doesn't look too happy," he said, but his smile told me he didn't care much.

"No, but I'm not sure he has a happy face, so I think we're good."

Sean laughed and stood abruptly, awkwardly juggling all the cards. "I'm sorry about the cards."

There was a grunt from the counter, although it was tough to tell if it was angry or conciliatory.

Sean placed them in front of Bob, "Would you like me to put them back? I'm afraid I won't do a good job."

Bob grunted again.

Sean reached for the largest box of candy in the display by the register. It was a gaudy gold foil heart-shaped box with fraying red paper lace around the edges, two graying red paper roses glued to the top, and a dusty, tacky red velvet-ish bow smack dab in the center. It was really a thing of 1970s velvet Elvis beauty. He looked up at Bob, "Can I get this, though?"

Bob's parchment skin folded over and over again into an origami smile. "Of course, although it's usually better to buy the lady her present before the date." I blushed a little as Bob then reached into the wire bin of bargain stuffed animals and pulled out a royal purple teddy bear, complete with tiny matching purple roses and a bow around its neck. Really, did everything in this shop have roses and a bow? The plushie's fabric fur was thin, and there was a comical tuft of troll doll hair on top. I wondered what Sean would do.

Sean took it and placed it on the box of candy, "You're right, of course, so something extra is definitely in order." He paid for the treasures, and he and Bob parted as unlikely allies. As he gingerly carried the items out the door, his elbow brushed the frame, and the bear started to slip. I reached for it, but he caught it in one fluid movement, "Uh uh, I haven't given it to you yet. How do you even know it's for you?" He grinned at me and then threw over his shoulder to Bob, "Some people's manners!"

Bob chuckled dryly as I blushed again. Mrs. Claus smiled as we walked past her, and I felt like the entire hospital was trying to make my first (second?) date a success. The thought struck me that my constant green companion might have something to do with all this goodwill, but I dismissed the thought as soon as I had it. That would require Larry to enter the hospital and then entreat human help. But still, I found myself looking at all the pastel décor, searching for the familiar flash of green.

We exited the spinning door and found ourselves in the warm afternoon air. The sun shone bright yellow, and the sky hung brilliantly overhead. The world seemed to have the same vivid coloring as the day I met Larry, the day my life changed. I blinked several times and wondered what was so different. Then I realized that in the last months of my life, I'd forgotten what happiness looks like.

"Nice," I said to Sean, "You actually got old Bob on your side."

"Oh, I knew after the first half hour that I was going to have to buy something. And after the second, I was pretty sure it would have to be big."

"So, the chocolates?"

"Would you believe they're one of the most expensive things there?"

"Oh, impressive!" I said, swatting his arm and rolling my eyes.

"That's right. My entire plan was to impress you with pricey old chocolates and grape Winnie."

"I love grape Winnie!" I said, reaching again for the little purple bear.

"Seriously, have you never received a present? You actually have to wait for the person to give it to you. That's how this works. Are you always this grabby?"

I faked a pout, "Have you ever given a present? You're actually supposed to give it at some point."

Sean laughed at that but still held onto the box and bear. "We haven't gotten to that part of the date yet.

"There's more to this date than a hospital gift shop and parking lot presents? Now I am impressed," I said, hiding my excitement under a careful layer of sarcasm. I found it so hard to believe that he had an actual plan.

His smile overshadowed the sun as he said, "Oh, you just wait."

I tried to fake irritation, but I was too absurdly happy to bother. "So, what's first on the agenda?"

Sean grinned wickedly and said, "Knocking over a hospital gift shop," as he abruptly spun on his heel and began walking back towards the hospital entrance. "You're on the lookout and getaway," he called over his shoulder.

Before I could respond, he turned around again. "You're not even trying," he said.

I smiled back at him, "I thought it best if we're not seen together. Raise suspicions and all."

He laughed and said, "Let's wait until later. I think Father Time in there goes to sleep by 7. We'll have the place to ourselves."

While he chuckled at his joke, I started for a moment. "Father Time?" Were we that well suited to each other? Did he have a manic leprechaun that granted terrible wishes? Or, more to the point, perfectly fine wishes granted in terrible ways?

Since I didn't join in the laughter, Sean stopped and looked at me strangely. "I was just kidding."

I blushed and smiled and then decided for a moment of total honesty, "I just thought it was odd you called him Father Time. That's what I think when I look at him. The Information Lady is Mrs. Claus…I don't actually remember her real name…" I trailed off lamely.

Sean's loud laugh was unexpected. "Mrs. Claus! Yes! That's totally her! Oh my gosh, that's great!"

I was happy some of the insanity that was my life was charming. Not all of it would be, but my new obsession with all things preternatural seemed to go over well. "It's just who she reminds me of. I honestly never noticed Bob until today. But Father Time felt accurate."

"Right?!?" Sean said, and we continued to his car.

He stopped in front of a bright red Hyundai Elantra hatchback. It was in good condition but obviously an older model. It made me smile. Sometimes, walking around the parking lot at our high school, I felt like mine was the only family that couldn't afford not just a car, but a brand-new SUV. I never blamed my mom for that. I think it was one of the few ways I was rational. The student parking lot was ridiculous, not my mom.

"Your chariot awaits," Sean said, and the door opened with a protesting squeak.

"Thank you, sir," I said haughtily and gracefully sat down. And then promptly lifted my legs up with a squeal. Dang vinyl seats in Arizona heat!

"Oh crap!" Sean said and quickly pulled me up. His face was red now, and after I was safely off the molten vinyl, he fumbled in the back seat for something. He re-emerged with a threadbare white cotton towel. His face was scrunched with embarrassment. "Sorry. Totally forgot."

I watched as he smoothed the towel over the passenger seat. He tried three times to get the towel to stay up on the back of the seat, finally giving up and folding it over on itself to form more of a cushion on the seat. Once these arrangements were settled, he turned back to me, "Ok, now your chariot awaits." I gave him a small grimace but slid gracefully once more into the seat. And this time, I stayed. Sean shut the door and sprinted to the driver's side.

"And now for the show."

~Chapter 22~

I was grinning like a maniac in the seat next to Sean. Sean was taking me on his tour of Phoenix. It wasn't something likely to make TripAdvisor, but I loved it. We left the hospital, got on the I-10 freeway, and made our way to the 7th Street Tunnel. He told me he had always loved going under that tunnel as a kid. In the brightness of day, it was a welcome refuge from the sun, and in the dark of night, it was a weirdly orange/yellow block of light. I laughed and told him that I had loved the tunnel ever since coming to the valley as well. He told me the trick was to hold your breath through the tunnel, and I told him that was for passing a graveyard. We didn't come to a consensus.

We continued our tour, with him pointing out sights that he liked. We passed the airport, and he told me that when the freeways were being redone, people used to be able to go to a certain spot and watch the planes take off and land. I couldn't imagine a Phoenix freeway without a thousand whizzing cars, but it sounded nice. He pointed out so many other sights, silly things, and funny memories that it made the whole city seem more magical and friendly.

He asked me once if I was bored, and I just shook my head. I would feel like a fool if I actually had to admit that I was loving this personal glimpse into the area. I also felt a little like a stalker in how much information I was filing away for later. He'd surely regret this entire thing if he knew that.

Finally, at a quarter to six, Sean announced that it was a good time for our gourmet dinner. I was having a great time and seeing the city in a whole new way, so I would have been fine waiting a few more hours, but I felt some slight hunger pangs in my stomach, so I agreed quickly.

"This…this is going to be great!" he said, grinning maniacally.

"I think you're putting too much pressure on dinner," I said, wondering if I was the sane one in the car.

"No, I mean actual dinner will be great," he said, glancing in the mirrors as he merged onto the crowded 101.

"Oh, you definitely know how to make a girl feel special," I said, smiling.

Sean's face went slightly red. "Dang it, Mary-Claire. Somehow you make me say the wrong thing all the time!"

I laughed. "Don't put this on me. You were talking long before I met you."

He groaned, "OK, dinner will be great. This date is amazing."

Now it was my turn to blush and change the subject. "So, you're kind of building up dinner. Where are we going?" I knew the Phoenix Valley was home to some amazing restaurants, and I was anxious and curious to see where we were going. I was semi-adventurous food-wise, but our current financial circumstances had not leant themselves to much dining out. There were quite a few food groups I had not yet tried.

Sean's smile got bigger, "Only my favorite restaurant in town. I'm hoping, since you're a transplant, that you haven't been there yet."

I couldn't help but smile back, "The suspense is killing me, c'mon, just tell me."

He got off the exit on Broadway and said, "Soon, I promise. It's just up the road."

I waited in silent impatience as he maneuvered through the thick Tempe traffic. It was the tail end of rush hour, and people were anxious for home. And angry, but angry seemed to be just a method of driving here some days. Maybe once I got a car and could drive, I would understand why, but for now, I just watched as cars jockeyed for an imaginary pole position.

We came to the light at McClintock and he turned left and then quickly right into a tight parking lot, a chorus of honks at the quick deceleration bidding us farewell from the roadway. He pulled into a parking space outside a definite fast-food-looking building. I wondered if this was a joke.

"Have you ever been to Ted's?" he asked, the excitement palpable in his voice.

I stared, first at the building and then at him. "Ted's? A hot dog place?" I desperately hoped the disappointment didn't show in my face. I knew it wasn't a joke; his face was too earnest for it to be. And so I felt deflated. I guess, in my mind, I was worth more than a hot dog. And now I knew I was not.

His enthusiasm had not deflated in the slightest, despite the fact that I knew I wasn't a good enough actress to hide how I was really feeling. "Don't worry," he said, "you'll love it! I promise. You have no idea how good a hot dog can be."

He jumped out of the car, and I followed suit. Another few cars had pulled into the parking lot behind us, and he was almost running to get ahead of them. I followed more slowly. Good grief, how much of a hurry was he in for a hot dog? He opened the glass door on the side, a couple of triumphant steps before another couple and I inched around them and…instantly hit a wall of people. The line literally began at this side door, and I couldn't even see the ordering counter.

Sean held the door for the other couple, who now had been joined by two other couples and a large group of teenagers, until the line moved enough for us to inch into the building. After all the irritation in the drivers' faces we had encountered on the way over, I expected the line to be about the same. But everybody in it seemed to share Sean's enthusiasm. I heard discussions both in front and behind us about what they were going to get and how exactly to top the dogs.

Once fully in the building, I noticed the aroma. As best as I can describe it, we were in an indoor barbeque, but the best kind. The smell of charring meat wafted from somewhere in front of us, mingled with deep-fried goodness. Slowly, I was coming around to his way of thinking.

Sean's face leaned in comfortably/uncomfortably close to mine. "Do you smell that? They are fire-grilling the dogs as we speak. Do you want me to order for you?"

I looked vaguely in his direction, trying to keep my lips from getting too close to his. "Yeah, sure. What am I getting?"

He craned his neck slightly, checking to see how far from the counter we were. We had shuffled a few more feet in. "I'll get a footlong, but I can get you a regular. We'll split the onion rings, and we can get drinks. I recommend the loganberry."

I nodded, then wrinkled my nose. "Um, you've kept me out a long time. I want a footlong too."

"Good for you, girl," the guy directly in front of us said and then turned back to his own discussion.

Sean laughed, "Of course you can have one. That's awesome!"

The line moved again, and I could see the counter. It was long, with a brick finish on the bottom and a green laminate counter and half wall. On the counter, nearest us were the usual condiments and cutlery trays. Behind the half wall, it looked like there were the usual fast food accouterments of fryer baskets and the like. The middle of the counter held a register, which was obviously where the food was to be picked up. But it was the far side of the counter that I noticed.

Fingers of fire licked up between cast iron grates. There were long dogs, short dogs, and a couple of different kinds of sausages. Next to the grill was some assortment of toppings for the dogs. The smell coming off the grill was insane. I was suddenly getting in the mood for a picnic.

"So, if you get all the toppings, it's ketchup, mustard, onions, relish, a pickle, and Ted's hot sauce. And sauerkraut, can't forget that!"

"No way," I said vehemently, "no sauerkraut."

Sean looked horrified, although I couldn't tell if it was exaggerated or not. "But that's how it's best!"

"With dirt on it?" I said, shaking my head.

"I'm with her," the woman behind us chimed in. The guy who approved my hot dog length nodded in approval.

"No way," the guy next to the woman said. "Purists know you have to have the kraut."

I had apparently started a lively debate around us. I was shocked to find that there were such strongly held opinions on the subject. I shrugged at Sean, "I didn't mean to start this, but no sauerkraut, or this date is over before we eat."

There was general laughter around, and Sean acquiesced. "Fine, fine, you can ruin yours by not having sauerkraut. But you better believe I'm getting it!"

This discussion had finally brought us within a few feet of the previously far end of the counter. The guy behind the grill pointed in our direction. Sean held up two fingers, "Two footlongs. An order of onion rings and two medium loganberries."

The guy behind the counter nodded, barked some orders, and threw two of the longest hot dogs I had ever seen on the grill. It was a fascinating, well-oiled machine that worked behind the counter. The two guys working the grill and taking orders worked together seamlessly. The main griller rolled dogs along the grill with precision, rotating them to charred perfection from one end of the grill to the other. By the time they got close to the toppings, they were crispy-skinned, with juices running down their sides. The juice would hit the grill, and flames would burst briefly.

We got right in front of the grill and our dogs were next, looking so perfect I could feel my mouth watering. I glanced briefly to the right and watched the other guy put on two more footlongs and a fat white sausage. I couldn't believe how much I was looking forward to a hot dog.

"How do you want them?"

"One with everything, including sauerkraut, one with just everything."

The speed with which he expertly slathered the dogs with the toppings was amazing. It only took him a matter of seconds to put all the condiments on one and lay the hot dog in the ruffled paper carrier. He finished dressing the second one before we had paid and gotten our other food. Now I looked around the crowded restaurant and wondered where we'd get a table.

"There's a few tables in the shade," Sean said, gesturing towards the side door through which we entered. The air was cooling down a little, so I nodded at him. I got ahead of him and pushed lightly between the crowd, creating a small opening for him to carry our loaded tray. I had the forethought to grab some napkins and straws as we went by.

He plunked the plastic tray on the table. "Dig in. Trust me, you don't get better than this."

I grabbed my footlong and took a bite. The skin actually cracked when I bit it, and juices dripped down my face and hand. The flavors mingled together perfectly, and the hot dog tasted like actual meat. It was truly delicious. I sighed and looked up at him, slightly embarrassed. I wiped my chin quickly with a napkin. Sean just smiled.

"Told ya," he said and then took a huge bite himself.

I tried to eat daintily, but it's nearly impossible with a foot-long hot dog, especially one dripping with toppings. And I am, in general, not a dainty girl. It's not my superpower. Or my lesser power. Or in my body at all. The other problem was this was probably the best hot dog I'd ever eaten. And I was hungry.

The onion rings were the perfect golden brown and really crispy. As I was sopping up ketchup with the last ring, I noticed him staring at me and smiling. I frowned slightly and popped the fried goodness into my mouth. I washed it down with a swig of loganberry drink and then said, "Am I doing this wrong?"

Sean laughed. "No, it's just I knew you'd like it…I just knew it! I am a little in awe of how fast you inhaled it. Seriously, don't most people chew?"

I laughed, too. "It was really good! And I've never been like 'most people'," I said, without thinking, and I almost missed when he said under his breath, "That's what I like the best."

~Chapter 23~

After dinner, I was feeling full and happy. A little too full...maybe the footlong had been a bit much. I glanced in the backseat at the wilting paper flowers on the boxed chocolate. Dust mites glittered above it in the quickly fading twilight sun. Before, I had sure been anxious to get my presents; now, I hoped it would be a while before he gave them to me. And I wasn't sure I wanted the chocolate at all.

"Hey, I know those are some super special gifts, but you seriously need to learn patience," Sean said. I returned my gaze to the front of the car and his comically upset face. "Do you try to spoil Christmas too?"

I made a face. "I hardly think that's the same category," I said. "My mom gets me presents from convenience stores, not hospital gift shops."

Sean was concentrating on navigating through the Phoenix freeway traffic, but I saw the corners of his eyes crinkle as he smiled. "Well, we're hardly at the convenience store level yet. Awfully full of yourself, aren't you?"

"I'm worth the very best," I said simply.

"Believe me, I am aware," he said, and I laughed.

"So, now, where are we off to?" I asked, truly content to watch the streetlights whizzing by. I was satisfied. I was happy. And I was no longer afraid to let this date go where it would.

"Another secret location," Sean said, and he seemed extra proud of himself.

"Jeez, do you work for the CIA or something," I said, fake grumbling to keep my bliss under wraps a little longer.

"Yup...oh crap. Now I've got to kill you. Or bring you into the organization. Or something. I'm really bad at the recruitment part of it. And the killing part. Really, I'm just good at the secrets."

"No, you're not," I said flatly, smugly pointing out the obvious.

"And there goes my whole career."

I chuckled, amazed at how easy it was to be with him. I had always assumed that if I ever got to this point, I would be a stuttering mess, unable to have a cogent conversation and for sure leaving him wishing he was anywhere else. But he was easy to talk to, and we shared the same weird sense of humor.

As I looked out the window, I saw the soft electric glow of a large building out my window. The edifice was huge and imposing in the near dark of twilight. I furrowed my brow, confused, as he turned up a palm tree-lined driveway towards what I now realized was one of the preeminent hotels in the area. A large fountain sent plumes of brightly lit spray into the night sky. He pulled around the circle to the front of the building. A valet rushed out and offered to take the car. And to his credit, he didn't wrinkle his nose at the old Hyundai.

Sean handed him the keys as grandly as if they were for a Lexus and grabbed my hand. He led me towards the quiet automatic doors, and I followed on legs growing more leaden with every step. Did he think I was so desperate to be with him that he could take me to a hotel on the first date? I mean, as hotels went, kudos to him, but still….

He walked into the lobby like he had every right in the world to be there, and no one gave us a second glance. We walked, no, strode, across the large, exquisite tile floor, past the long reception desk. One clerk looked up briefly at us, and I thought we'd be asked to leave. But Sean didn't even acknowledge her, and she took no further notice.

As we got to a carpeted hallway, Sean leaned over to me, "The trick in a place like this is to act like we have a perfect right to be here. If you look worried, they notice you. If you act like you don't care, they think you belong."

I looked at him, thoroughly confused. "Do we not belong here?"

Sean smiled, "Here? I doubt I'll ever actually belong here. But just wait, you'll love this!"

He went past the bank of elevators, past several opulent-looking convention rooms. He seemed to know where he was going, but I was curious and nervous. I felt distinctly out of place in the splendor, but Sean didn't seem bothered by it at all. And, true to his word, as he breezily walked by employees and guests, no one seemed to notice us either. It's quite possible we weren't worth noticing, but I couldn't help but feel that if we were skulking around, looking like we were afraid of getting caught, we'd definitely be noticed.

We walked down several hallways on velvety carpet. The walls were a tasteful beige, which I somehow recognized as being different and, truthfully, better than normal beige. They exuded style and sophistication instead of just generic-ness. The door and wall trimmings were all white and marble-y, which somehow made the beige doors feel coolly monochromatic. I was definitely out of my element. I slowed a little. It wasn't the greatest feeling, the one of not belonging at all, and it was one with which I was all too familiar. Sean didn't seem to notice my discomfort--or if he did, just like it had all night, his own enthusiasm more than made up for my misgivings--but he did notice I had begun to lag behind.

Flashing his patented smile, he grabbed my hand to hurry me forward. My feet propelled my body faster, but my mind was focused on his warm grip—and my mind liked it. Luckily, my feet had been learning how to function independently for the last few months, so they just kept doing what they did, and eventually, we found ourselves at a bank of elevators.

There were a few people gathered in front of the doors. They glanced at us but then away again. We weren't worth their time. I wondered where we were going. I had thought we might be going out a back door to explore the gardens or something, but I didn't see an exit, and it seemed highly unlikely that we would access the gardens from anything but the ground level. And he was hanging back, a little further behind the cluster of people than felt absolutely necessary. Not knowing what to expect was becoming almost mundane at this point. I shrugged inwardly and just let him hold my hand. The important thing was he had grabbed my hand several minutes ago and had yet to drop it.

The golden elevator doors opened, and the usual assortment of fancy people got off, and the next batch of similarly fancy people stepped in. I went to move forward, but he applied subtle pressure to my hand, so I stopped. A guy held the elevator door for us, but out of the corner of my eye, I saw Sean shake his head slightly and tilt it towards me, first puckering and then with a big grin. The man smiled back and let the doors close. We were alone in the corridor.

"What was that?" I asked him, wanting to yank my hand away, but my arm stubbornly refused.

"What?" he asked innocently, suddenly on the move towards the stair door I hadn't noticed before. It was beige, of course, but without trim, like it was a servant door, necessary but unwelcome, and needed to blend in.

"What was that secret signal you exchanged with the elevator man?"

Sean laughed, pushing open the door. "I didn't want to make too big a fuss about not taking the elevator. Strictly speaking, I'm not entirely sure where we're going to is a hundred percent sanctioned by the hotel. Best not to call attention to ourselves."

That stopped me. Well, more accurately, that stopped my arguments. He still held my hand, and my body was politely moving me up the stairs to keep my hand attached. But now I was truly wondering what was going on. Where were we headed that we shouldn't be?

"Um, look, it's been great, but seriously, I can't get into trouble. I mean, I can't."

Sean paused on the 2nd-floor landing and looked at me. "Oh, Mary-Claire, I'm sorry. I like a good mystery, but I didn't think of how this looks. I've been here plenty of times. We're not breaking in anywhere. I've just never asked permission, so I just don't know. But they wouldn't have put in access if they didn't want us going, right?"

He started up the next flight of metal steps—all luxury and lavishness on the outside, total utilitarian on the inside—and I followed. The phrase "access" stuck in my mind, and I noticed on the next landing that there was a sign declaring "No Roof Access." It was the door by this sign that he stopped and pushed, almost timidly, peeking out. Then he opened it wide, and we came back into the grand world where I didn't belong, but only briefly.

There was another door right next to the one we exited, and he pushed that open quickly, probably because there was a soft thump of an elevator door stopping. The heavy metal door clicked quietly into place as I heard the doors of the elevator sliding open.

We started up the next set of stairs, but not before I noticed the sign "Roof Access." We climbed another three floors. I was no longer as concerned about where we were going as much as when we would get there. I was desperately trying to slow my breathing. I wasn't totally out of shape, but neither was I in the best of shape. Sean didn't seem to notice the ascent, but I was beginning to count every step, praying that each one would be the last. Finally, it was.

We were at the top, or what I could only assume was the top. We were facing a cement wall--they really didn't try to spice up the innards of the building--and another metal door. The only other way to go was back down the stairs, and I have to admit, as much fun as the previous adventures had been, if this part of the date was stair running, he could take me home, hand holding or no hand holding. Speaking of that, he dropped my hand, grinned at me, and used both hands to triumphantly open the last door.

We exited the building into the cool crisp Phoenix night. There was the general hum of the city in the air, but the noise was muted, more white noise than cacophony. I stepped gingerly on the graveled roof, unwilling to add noise to calm. It was no use, but my sneakers only made the softest crunch as I walked. It was dark, the looming mountain behind the hotel was lit with floodlights, but none of it was reflected to us. In fact, the mountain seemed to swallow the light the way it drank the sun in during the day. I was now thoroughly puzzled. What were we doing up here? I turned to ask Sean, but he was rounding the small square of a building that housed the door; I didn't follow quickly. His contagious enthusiasm somewhat diluted in the quiet dark of the roof.

"Mary-Claire," he said from somewhere in the darkness. "Trust me one more time."

I frowned at the artificially lit mountainside and looked for wisdom from the shadow-draped cacti. Oddly, I gleaned nothing helpful from their spiny forms. Trust him one more time tonight. Or, for one last time, I thought I should just leave. Just go quickly through the door and escape in an Uber. I could keep my promise not to let Larry get his way. I would be alone again at school. I should just go...

I frowned at the small expanse of lit desert. The wisdom of the ancients wasn't flowing tonight. And I had very little wisdom of my own. And no self-control. And I was tired of being lonely. I turned from the vista, looked briefly at the door, and walked toward his voice.

"Just look," he said as I came around the part of the building that had been blocking my view. He was illuminated like a circus emcee, with a seemingly endless array of glittering lights behind him. I gasped quietly. It felt like the entirety of the Valley of the Sun lay before me.

Valley of the Sun in the day, but tonight it was a Valley of a Million Stars. A galaxy of lights, running the gamut from brilliant orange to bright white, shimmered with untold, unknown constellations hidden in its beauty. When we had driven in, I had noticed the light-lined palm tree drive, but I hadn't noticed the vast expanse of lawn on either side. In the cover of night, from our perch on the top of the hotel, it was an island of dark, giving needed contrast to the almost overwhelming array. It was dazzling.

"I told you," he said, stepping to the side and gesturing for me. I walked slowly toward him, entranced by a city I felt I had never really seen before. Interspersed between all the orange, yellow, and white were bright pockets of neon color. All the restaurants, all the gas stations, everything added to the symphony of light. I stood next to him, admiring the bustling city from above, loving the feeling of life and enjoying the oasis of calm.

"Um…" I said, not knowing what exactly to say. "It's stunning."

He laughed softly next to me and gently put his hand on mine. I felt the now familiar jolt in my arm, but other than that, it felt completely natural—and all the more so when he gently squeezed it. I obviously had little to compare it to, but the night felt nearly perfect. I leaned my head against his shoulder and was very happy when he not only didn't pull away but moved in slightly closer.

We stood in silence for what felt like forever and just a few moments, all at the same time. The bustle of millions of people played out in near silence before us. It was moving art. Light pollution is decried, with good reason, but now with its perfect inky, velvet backdrop, the lights were an electric parade moving before us. After a while, although the silence was very comfortable between us, I felt almost a need to talk. I looked away briefly from the scene before me and up at him.

"This has all been perfect, seriously, but I don't feel like I know you any better," I said. "Tell me something about you. What's your family like?"

"Oh, you know, typical, I guess. It's me, my two sisters, and my parents. It's a boringly good life. For the most part," he seemed to hesitate. "I guess I just try to live up to my dad's expectations too much." Now his voice got lower, "I mean, I like football, I guess, but if it were up to me, I would sing in the choir. But my dad wouldn't have that, not his only son!"

"Really?" I asked, surprised.

Then his shoulder started shaking. "No, sorry. I couldn't help it. My life is just too boring." He was laughing. I punched his shoulder, and he smiled down at me. "I mean, the first part is true. I have two sisters. But my parents are cool. My dad is actually the one who took me to my first musical and my first football game. He likes everything. He has a great tenor."

I pursed my lips. "Is that the truth? Why would you tell such a ridiculous story?"

He smiled as he said, "It felt more in the moment. You know, like an after-school special."

I stared at him. Nobody but me seemed to use that phrase.

"You know what an after-school special is?"

He looked chagrined. "No, not really. It's something my mom says to my sisters when they're being dramatic. I like the way it sounds. Do you know what it means?"

"As a matter of fact, my mom told me once, so I do."

"Please explain."

I smiled. "Once, a long time ago, you couldn't come home from school and watch whatever you wanted."

"Ohh, the Dark Ages!" he said with exaggerated solemnity.

I shook my head, "No, not even close. Seriously, there was nothing on when kids got home from school."

"Dark Ages."

"Stay in school. So the powers-that-used-to-be would every now and then have a TV show on in the afternoon for kids. Only it wasn't entertaining; it was a moral story."

"See, now, this whole morality play really sounds Dark Age-ish," he said insistently.

I rolled my eyes and said, "You really need to pay more attention in history class."

"No, I think I pay the perfect amount of attention," he said, smiling. "And don't think I missed the eye roll!"

I blushed and hoped there was enough darkness to cover for me. "Anyway," I said, dragging the word out dramatically, "the story would be about some teen who experienced trouble in any of the following areas: drug use, alcohol, eating disorder, bad friends, you know the drill. In the end, they would learn some lessons. Thus, the watching teens would also learn said lessons."

"I'm getting crap for the Dark Ages, and you used the word 'thus'? This seems unfair. It's also unfair that now you know all about the mundane existence I call life, and I know nothing about you."

I sighed and settled my head against his shoulder again. I didn't want to admit how much I would give for boring. "I was bored too until about a year ago. And I guess I'm just another statistic. My dad decided that being married wasn't his thing. And apparently, older kids weren't his thing, either. He left us, hooked up with some twenty-something waitress, knocked her up, and will probably marry her. Oh, and just for good measure, they moved to New York." I knew I sounded more bitter than I had intended. It was just that I realized at the moment it was the first time, the very first time, that I had told anybody about it. I had no close friends, and my mom and brother already knew what was happening. Who would I tell? Despite the bitterness, it felt great. I had admitted the most shattering thing to happen to me so far, and I was still standing. Without waiting for him, I laced my fingers with his.

We stood in silence for a little longer, then he said, "I'm sorry. I didn't know. I shouldn't have joked about my family." I was surprised he didn't wonder, even briefly, if I was telling the truth. But he didn't, and I was glad I didn't make up some lame story. And I really couldn't think of anything that sounded much worse than what I had gone through last year. I mean, I know there is worse, but for my personal story, it felt pretty bad. "It's ok. I liked the joke. And we got the history lesson about 'after school special,' so I feel like it was a win all around."

His free hand began to stroke my arm, and I felt his head incline more towards mine. Oh good grief, was he leaning in? I had heard about leaning in. I knew the pop culture references. And I knew where it was heading. And I couldn't go there. The night had been perfect, oh crap, too perfect. Larry! He was here. He had to be here. That was the only excuse for all of this.

Please brain, do something, I thought desperately. And it did, something horrible and mood-killing, good little brain. "So, exactly how many girls have you brought up here?"

Sean stiffened. Froze really, his fingers going from pliable to pillar in a nanosecond. I looked up at him and was surprised by the look on his face. It was both shocking and sad. What had I said and why?

To his credit, he didn't yank his hand away, but I knew I had effectively killed any more leaning in tonight. "Actually, only one," he said, both sorrowfully and stiffly. And I knew, I knew, who it was. Tessa. Well, perfect. That's just perfect. Date, officially over.

"I'm sorry. I blurt things when I get nervous," I said, blurting something because I was nervous. "I..."

Sean's hand thawed in mine. He gave me a little squeeze. "It's ok. At least I know you're not the cool man-killer you come off, and now we're even about the family joke." He was quiet for a moment, and then he continued, "Yes, it was Tessa. I love it up here, and I don't like the idea of sharing it with just anybody. I'm always afraid of coming up here and finding a crowd. She liked it too. I really think you two would like each other. Once any and all awkwardness was out of the way."

I like the way he used the present tense with Tessa. Even though the mention of her had definitely killed the vibe going on, it still felt comfortable between us. But the time on the roof had come to an end. We both seemed to sense that at the same time. As we turned away from the view, I wondered if I would return, and would it be with Sean or just alone. Again.

~Chapter 24~

I thought the car ride back would be excruciatingly bad. I was so proud of myself for spoiling the moment, but also really, really disappointed. It was the right thing. It really was. Right...?

We waited for the valet, not really speaking. He brought the car and was both surprised and pleased with the tip Sean gave him. We got in, and Sean said, "They're always so good here. They take the 'Dai and park it like it's some impressive car. I appreciate that. It's all my parents will give me to drive, but I want the world to know I know how to treat people."

Better than I do. The more I thought about the inappropriateness of my question, the worse I felt. My brain really couldn't have found any other way to break the spell? Bringing up the comatose ex-girlfriend was overkill, plain and simple. C'mon brain, work with me a little.

I was so absorbed in my stupidity that I wasn't paying much attention to Sean. Suddenly, by the fountain, which, of course, had a pullout, the car stopped.

"Mary-Claire, I'm such a dope."

That caught my attention.

He got out of the car, and I scrambled after him. I looked around, wondering what sight he was showing me now. I was staring into the unlit expanse of lawn beyond the brightly lit palm trees when I felt him tug on my arm.

I turned and he was close by, and I could see wilting flowers and the ridiculous bear and chocolates peeking out from behind his back. I had almost forgotten my aging bounty.

One corner of his mouth tugged upwards, "I think now is the perfect time to give you your gifts." I looked at my toes, perplexed. I really thought I'd messed things up but good on the rooftop.

He put a hand under my chin and pulled my face up so I looked directly into his eyes. "Mary-Claire, it's ok. It's ok to be nervous, and it's ok to talk about Tessa. Yes, it makes me sad, but honestly, we were probably coming to an end. And both of us felt the same. We'd actually talked about it a time or two before...anyway. It's ok."

He let go of my face, looked away and was quiet for a moment. I wondered if I should say anything, stay silent or order myself an Uber. I had nearly decided on the last option when he shook his head, looked at me and spoke again, maybe not as cheerfully as normal, but definitely more upbeat than before.

"And now, madame," he said with an exaggerated flourish of his arm, "Here you go. Grape Winnie and the oldest box of chocolate known to exist."

I looked into his eyes, and although I saw some sadness in them, I also saw happiness. I decided to let the night go where it may, so I laughed and eagerly grabbed at them. The purple bear was even more forlorn up close. The "fur" felt like little more than tufts of lint stuck to felt. It was threadbare in spots and had bald patches throughout. And it smelled. Not like grapes. Not like grapes at all.

The packaging for the chocolates disintegrated as I tried to pry it up. It was undoubtedly a sign of what was to come. The chocolate had the mottled white look of candy that had experienced a bad temperature change—which I knew was normal and didn't mean the candy was bad—but the effect made them look like they were graying with age.

Sean looked at me with a wicked grin, "I dare you to eat one. Just one."

I looked at him and shook my head, "Only if you do first. I need to know they're not poisoned."

He laughed, "I guess food poisoning is still poisoning."

His fingers hovered over the graying confectionaries. He screwed up his mouth and finally chose one with what definitely looked like an almond hidden under the aging chocolate. "Go at the same time?"

I studied the contents of the box and finally chose the least objectionable item I could see, which, oddly, was the smallest piece in the box.

Sean counted down, "Three, two, one," and we both took a bite. This decision made my untimely question on the roof look like a wise choice. It was a contest to the end to see who would finish the whole thing. Sean won. Mine ended up in the bushes. The entire episode lightened the mood considerably, and the car ride to my apartment was back to the same easy back-and-forth that had been the vein of the evening.

We pulled into my apartment parking lot. The night had finished so well, and most of the date had been so great, that everything had taken on a different sheen. The dirty off-white stucco gleamed pearlescent in the moonlight. The dull, dark red tiles on the roof seemed to shine with an otherworldly glow. We got out of the car, and he started walking me to my door. I saw a faint light, probably a lamp from the family room, in the large window at the front of our condo. I held the precious purple bear in one hand, leaving my other one hanging precariously free and close to his. It was now officially as important to me as the tiny turquoise ring in the box upstairs. The patchy fur and ridiculous color made it all the more precious.

The parking lot was completely quiet. More so than I had ever noticed it. All our neighbors seemed to be in for the night. That felt slightly odd, but I have to admit, I'm not out late as a general rule, so I supposed it was possible. The white lines delineating the parking spaces shone, almost neon, almost too bright. I looked around the oddly lit lot and noticed how everything appeared to have the same sparkly sheen. I glanced at the sky and noticed for the first time that the moon was unusually large tonight. It was a Bruce Almighty moment, and for the first time, I got that scene in the movie. Everything seemed magical.

Magical! That thought brought me up sharply, and I looked around the parking lot. I'm not sure how I expected to see a Smurf-sized being in the dim light; even a giant moon only produces so much illumination. I scanned under parked cars, looked deeply into the scrub that passed for landscaping, and glanced at my apartment. Nothing. He was probably still sleeping it off or out, trying to find a luckless fairy for a Middle Earth fling.

"Mary-Claire?"

I jumped and realized that in my attempt to find Larry, I neglected my date. Had Sean been talking the whole time? Sheepishly I looked at him and said, "Yes?"

"Do you even know the question I asked you?" He asked it with a knowing smile, and I blushed.

"Of course," I said brightly, straining my eyes just across the darkness one more time, just to be sure.

"So, you agree then?"

"What? Um, yes?"

His smile grew, and then he said, "Well, great. It's settled. You pay for all the rest of the dates we go on, and I get to pick where we go. I never thought I'd get any girl to agree to that, but since you're okay with it..."

I laughed out loud then. I couldn't help it. He looked so proud of himself, and the way his eyes sparkled when he teased me was mesmerizing. I deliberately chose not to focus on the "rest of the dates" remark and instead tackled the totally wrong pact I had apparently made. "I don't think that will hold up in court. There are several mitigating factors."

"Really?" he said, going along with it, "like what exactly?" He leaned in close, his mouth a stern line, but his eyes danced with moonlit amusement.

Like your face, I thought. Like your smile, your laugh, your eyes. Like, I'm too happy right now to disagree with anything. It felt a little like being drunk, I guess. Was there such a thing as being too happy to consent?

"The moonlight. It's a little too bright. It hurts my eyes, and I can't think straight." Not my best, but I couldn't actually say what I was thinking, could I? As I've stated before, sometimes my brain stem works better than others.

"I object. I don't think that's a valid reason."

"Like you know...I've watched more Judge Judy than you."

"Ah, but I'm a Law & Order scholar sooo..." His teeth gleamed in the moonlight. He was trying so hard not to smile, to stay in lawyerly character, but the corners of his mouth twitched adorably. Dang him.

"Objection, your honor, teasing the witness," I said, finally making him break character and laugh. I'd been fighting all night to not give in, to not let Larry win. I thought of the top of the hotel. I had been successful under great odds, but I lost at this very moment. I was done. I was hopelessly falling for him, Larry be damned. I mean, I had fallen for him long ago; it was the cause of this whole mess. But before, I liked what I saw, and the few interactions I had had with him. Now, as I was beginning to know him, I knew I had fallen hard, and he was all I had dreamt he would be.

I had expected some new crushing guilt at this moment, but it didn't come. Hurting Tessa had gotten him exactly what I wanted. My wish…or was it? I had fallen completely for Sean, but that wasn't the wish. I was already halfway there when I'd made it. The wish had been for Sean to be mine. I didn't know how to feel now. Part of me desperately hoped that he was not feeling the same. What more could I do than I had done tonight? Larry certainly couldn't fault my performance. What if it wasn't enough, what if he didn't fall for me?

But that thought was hardly comforting either. What if he didn't fall for me? I had been at my best tonight. I knew I looked pretty good tonight. I was funny and personable. If Sean didn't like me, that was all on me. Larry had admitted that he couldn't make Sean fall in love with me. So, if he wasn't feeling anything tonight, then I wasn't as lovable as I'd hoped. What did that mean for me? Honestly, would nothing ever be easy?

"Alright, I give. You can pick the next one, or two, or three." Sean's eyes finally caught mine. I didn't look away. His lips twitched at the corners, and he leaned in. Softly, quickly, his lips met mine. "Or four or five. I think you're going to win all the arguments from now on." And he kissed me again. This time he lingered on my lips, and I felt his fingers caressing my chin. When he broke the kiss, his face stayed close, and he smiled.

We started towards the front door again, his fingers intertwined with mine. Neither of us spoke, but it wasn't awkward or uncomfortable at all—until I looked up at my window. I had meant to look towards the sky, but my gaze was arrested by the prominent green flash in the window. Fully outlined in the moonlight was a maniacally grinning miniature man. Even from this distance, even in the inky dark, I could have sworn his eyes sparkled like two fiery emeralds. And he looked triumphant.

~Chapter 25~

I don't actually remember what I said to leave. I was both caught up in the kiss and horrified by the glimpse of the Irish demon. I was reasonably sure that I bowed out somewhat gracefully. At least, my last snapshot of Sean was him at my front door, smiling that lopsided smile I couldn't get enough of and saying, "I'll call you tomorrow," before giving me one last quick kiss. Then mercifully, sadly, he was gone.

I entered the apartment intending to find Larry and have it out with him. I wanted to make sure he knew he hadn't won, although I was pretty sure my arguments would all be weak. But he couldn't think he had been responsible. Maybe if he wasn't, it would be a small loophole I could hang my pride on. I might have fallen for Sean, he might have fallen for me, but it was natural and not the work of the Emerald Gremlin.

Before I could head upstairs, my mom walked out of the family room. She looked happily at me.

"Dinner lasted a while. That's got to be a good sign," she said, grinning her pre-divorce smile. I hadn't seen it in so long, and I realized I had to stop to talk to her. She deserved whatever joy she could find in life, especially given the last few days.

"Yeah..." I said, trying to play it cool, but honestly, when has cool ever been my strong suit? "It was so awesome, Mom!"

She rushed over, hugged me, and then motioned for me to sit in a chair at the table. I threw one last desperate glance at the stairs and then sat down. She pulled out milk and Oreos, and I briefly wondered where the cameras were. Surely we were filming a commercial. But I let the snarky thoughts die in my brain for once; she looked so pleased and at ease that I couldn't help but get caught up in it.

"Tell me all about it," she said as she dunked an Oreo.

I told her all about the date, where we went, what we ate. She seemed especially interested in the part of the Phoenician roof. She asked so many questions about it and then smiled and said she thought she'd make a trip up there herself.

"So, Mary-Claire, is this going to be a more regular thing?" she asked, trying for nonchalance, but I could see the hope in her eyes and could almost read the thought in her mind, one of us should be happy.

I tried to play it off as well. "Maybe..." I said the word trailing off, but I knew I was smiling and blushing, so I finished, "I mean, he did say I could pick the next three or four places we go."

She clapped her hands and beamed at me. The noise roused Mike from his gaming in the other room, and he came in, grabbed a couple of Oreos, and sat down. "Whacha smiling about?" he said, teeth covered in slimy black crumbs.

"Your sister had a good night," Mom said.

"Don't talk with your mouth full," I said.

Mike opened his mouth and stuck out his food-covered tongue. "Is this bad?"

I stifled a giggle, Mom flicked his forehead, and he laughed, spewing cookie crumbs all over.

"And that's why," my mom said as she went to the sink for a sponge.

Mike grinned at me across the table.

It felt so easy and natural, and I wanted to stay wrapped in the family glow forever, but up the dark stairs lurked the nightmare I needed to face.

"I'm tired, Mom," I said and rose from the table. She smiled at me, "I'm sure you are sweetheart. It seems unnecessary to say, but sweet dreams."

I kissed her cheek quickly, messed with Mike's hair, and trudged up the stairs. I would normally have turned on a light, but I found myself hoping that I had imagined what I had seen in the window, that Larry was either not there or asleep, and I didn't want to alert him to my presence just in case that gloriously became the truth. Still nestled in the warmth of my family, I was beginning to doubt that I had actually seen Larry. I mean, what were the odds that I could even see him from the parking lot, in the dark, when he was upstairs? It seemed far more likely I had imagined him out of guilt. My steps became lighter almost instantly.

I entered my room and glanced around. And saw nothing. I sighed and collapsed on my bed, letting my mind wander through the best parts of the evening. I knew I was smiling a ridiculous smile, but no one was around to see it, so I gave in.

"Ah Mary-Claire, 'tis good to see ye smile."

I bolted upright and saw him sitting idly on my windowsill. His tiny face radiated pleasure and satisfaction. And I knew he had been in the window earlier.

"Can't I just enjoy this for a minute without you ruining it?" I asked, my irritation evident, but he looked unbothered by it.

"Enjoy, Colleen, please do. I do not mean to interrupt you."

I looked at him cautiously. He looked so proud, like this was all his doing. I knew he wasn't thinking of the horror he had put Tessa's family through. And I felt anger well up inside of me. "This wasn't your doing," I said, hoping to wipe the gloating grin off his face. "None of your schemes worked."

He hopped lazily off the sill and onto my dresser. He seemed to be waltzing across the top towards me, and all the while, the smug smile stayed the same. The backward baseball cap from earlier in the day now rakishly set to the side. He looked very pleased with himself.

"Oh, wasn't it lassie? Did all my schemes fail? How will I live with meself?" he said, the Irish brogue sounding musical. He definitely didn't seem defeated.

"Yes...no...I mean.." I said, trying to sound confident, but it came out as anything but. I was confused, he was sure, and I hated it.

"Certainly, the gust of wind that blew your papers came out of nowhere, right?" he said. He had arrived at my nightstand and was looking directly into my eyes. He looked amiable enough, and there was no hint of guile or amusement.

"The wind," I said softly, thinking back to my first interaction with Sean after the accident. I had looked; I remembered looking! I hadn't seen Larry anywhere. A gust of wind outside wasn't so abnormal. That didn't have to be him, it could have been just the weather. I felt sure he was trying to take credit for nature, and I settled back on my pillows. And then it hit me, it had to be him. I had never admitted to him that I had spoken to Sean on that day. There would be no way for him to know about it if he wasn't there. And if he was there, then the gust could have easily come

from him. I got off my bed and went closer to him. I looked directly
into his eyes. "So, the wind, but that's not…" I began, but his smile
grew and stopped.

"And the time at the hospital when the clock stopped
working," he said. I gaped at him, wanting desperately to find
something in his face that I could grab onto and make the dawning
realization go away.

"You hate hospitals," I said weakly, and I heard how pathetic
I sounded.

"Honestly Mary-Claire, I was surprised you fell for that one.
You seemed much smarter than that. There's nothing in your world
that bothers me. I thought for sure you would recognize that, so I
did. But you believed what you wanted to believe." The baseball cap
was changed for the nurse's cap again, and he smiled, "I actually find
hospitals soothing. At night, they can be very quiet. I sat with Tessa
meself at times. I watched over her for you."

I went to sit on my bed, missed, and collapsed on the floor. I
felt utterly defeated, all the more so because I knew I wouldn't go
back and undo what he had done. Not now. If I had realized sooner, I
told myself, I would absolutely have put a stop to things. But now,
now when Sean had kissed me, now when we had connected, and
now when I had Tessa's own mother's blessing.

I felt a light pressure on my leg. Larry stood there looking
earnestly up at me. "I am sorry, Colleen. Not for granting your wish,
I'll not be sorry for that. But I am sorry you are so upset. If it makes
you feel any better, I did not follow you in the hospital at first. I
thought I would just let you be. But then I saw Sean coming in one
day right after you left. And I knew I had to do something. I knew
you were an honest one, so I did. You would keep your word and not
try to meet up with him." The nurse's cap disappeared and was
replaced with a crown, gold with a giant green buckle in the front.
This little fool knew he was the king of tonight, and it made me ill.

I wanted to fling him across the room, but in the midst of my
emotional turmoil, I found his words were more comforting than I
expected. Although I thought little of his own integrity, he
apparently thought highly of mine. I looked at him intently, and he
stared right back. Neither of us spoke.

Finally, he said, "I will admit, although I will be denying it if
ye tattle, but I did feel a wee bit bad about the girl Tessa. She looked

so pale in the hospital, she did. I maybe, just maybe, mind ye, could have found another way. But I didn't. And that's that."

I stared at him, my anger, sadness, and horror softening. He wasn't lying. "So, you wouldn't do it the same?" I asked, desperate for some proof he had changed. I had two more wishes to get through.

He looked at me and shrugged his tiny shoulders. "I dunno. Tis hard to say. I might have tried to find another way, but if I could not, then yes, I would do it all again. Although I think I would have tried to lessen the fall."

I leaned against my bed and thought about what he said. In the time we'd been together, I had come to the undeniable realization that he did not understand humans. And he lacked the essential feeling of empathy that would have enabled him to care. But just now, he had admitted that he felt bad, a "wee bit," about Tessa, and he said he might have tried to find another way. Was this progress? It was going to have to be because, for now, our fates were intertwined.

I looked at him intently. "Larry, I'll tell you now. I'm scared to wish again. And, while I do admit I've kind of gotten used to you, I know we both want you back on your rainbow. So, you need to promise me that no matter what else I foolishly wish, you won't physically hurt another person."

Larry looked back with equal intensity, "That is a hard thing to promise. But this has been too much of a fight. I like you too, lass. I'll be happy when I'm back in my own home, but I do believe I will think of you once in a while by name. That may not sound like much, but I canna remember a single other name of any human I've met. All that being said, I do solemnly promise you that I will not physically hurt another of you great beasts again."

I smiled at him, the first true smile I'd given him in a few days. "Shake on it?"

He reached over and shook my pointer finger with one tiny hand. "Truth be told, I think this might be interesting. I'll have to think of different ways of getting things done."

I felt slightly uneasy at that, wondering how many people the serial killer Larry had put in an early grave in his quest to fulfill wishes.

"One more thing. Were you actually drunk today?"

Larry started laughing at that one. "Ah, Mary-Claire. D'ya actually think I could put together such a smashing outfit as I did today if I was blathered? No, I did tell you the truth. I never work after imbibing. You just didn't listen. That's the trouble, I'll be thinking. You need to pay better attention to the rules and your next wish."

www.ingramcontent.com/pod-product-compliance
Lightning Source LLC
Chambersburg PA
CBHW071917220626
47052CB00002B/391